Rob Lofthouse was born in Twickenham and joined his local county infantry regiment (1 PWRR) straight from school at the age of sixteen. After serving 20 years, having served in Poland, Germany, Kenya, Canada, Falkland Islands, Iraq, Northern Ireland, and Kosovo, he retired in the rank of Sergeant.
Rob lives on the south coast with his wife and three children.

**Bazooka Town**

**By**

**Rob Lofthouse**

## FOREWORD BY MAJOR JUSTIN FEATHERSTONE MC

The narrative of war places a stark and often disquieting lens on the tensions between social identity and humanity. In 'Bazooka Town', Robert Lofthouse again uses his deep personal insight as a former infantry Sergeant and combat veteran to create the carefully-crafted characters at the heart of this irregular band of guerrilla fighters operating in the deepening shadows of the final stages of the war in Europe.

The original Operation Werewolf led to the training of a commando force by Obergruppenführer Prützmann, which by early 1945 comprised of probably no more than two hundred soldiers, largely drawn from the Hitler Jugend. This largely ineffectual organisation was more of a propaganda tool, and proved of no subsequent military significance, but with these particular characters such as Dieter and Thomas would have drawn inspiration from Joseph Goebbels' 'Werewolf Speech' of 23rd March 1945, in which he called for all native Germans to fight to the death, in a demonstration of resistance to the advancing Allied armies.

Erik's experiences of fighting resonate deeply and reflect the confusion, horror, desperation and intimacy of close combat, the reader is propelled in to the maelstrom, and it is possible to feel that you are genuinely at the side of this young soldier.

The escalation of partisan activity from ambushes and close-quarter assassinations, to the murder of civilians and the abhorrent treatment of prisoners, is both shocking and rapid. The question of why essentially good men can become so morally degenerate is at the core of this book.

'Bazooka Town' is multi-layered, relentless, relevant and powerful. As a detailed and rigorously related narrative of a broken irregular unit fighting a desperate and futile insurgent action, it is both dramatic and engrossing. As a study of the insidious impact on moral agency by social identity and social structure, it is even more deeply affecting. Dehumanisation of the German soldiers involved, and the transition from regular soldiers to brigands capable of acts of barbarism provokes moral outrage. This erosion of humanity is even more marked as witnessed by Erik, who although traumatised, resists the corrupting effect of what the others view as an existential fight. For the other Werewolves, national survival and dignity are causes that supersede the accepted conventions of both war and morality; the attrition caused by the years of fighting within a Total War environment have led to them losing the touchstones of perceived decency and sense of self worth clash of a sacrosanct, incorrigible moral core, and the resolute adherence to an ideology and desire for survival that eclipses all governed and rational behaviours, both on and away from the field of battle. It is this very idea that remains the foundation of professional military ethos and discipline; as much to protect the mental wellbeing of individual soldiers, as to prevent acts of inhumanity in an environment where humanity itself remains so fragile.

This nuanced and arresting portrait of the tensions between a soldier's sense of self, agency, identity and morality, is framed with integrity, and a genuine understanding that can only come from a soldier's heart. These ideas remain as conflicted and tested today in modern military operations.

To all who suffered and endured during those dark times.
1939-1945

Only the dead have seen the end of war.

-Plato

## AUTHORS NOTE

Officially, open hostilities between allied and the German Armed Forces ended on 7th May 1945. You would be forgiven that as far as the European Theatre of Operations was concerned, the war was over. In fact, for the majority, this was true. What was also a fact was the continued resistance of certain German forces well beyond 1945.

Not unlike what Coalition forces faced in both Iraq and Afghanistan recently, the Allied occupying forces faced a grave threat from certain insurgent factions comprising of Pro-Nazi citizens, Waffen SS, Hitler Youth, and a small number of Werhmacht, Kriegsmarine, and Luftwaffe personnel. Despite the formal surrender of the German Armed Forces on 7th may, there were many small groups of German forces who ignored such a declaration and continued to fight on regardless. Radio communications in April –May 1945 were limited at best between German Command locations and their fighting units.

Hienrich Himmler, leader of the SS, considered the possibility of an insurgent force operating behind enemy lines as they occupied Germany itself. Himmler was without ceremony berated by Hitler for considering such an idea. To promote an insurgency, in Hitler's' mind was to admit that his Armed Forces were losing. He dismissed Himmler's' idea out of hand, and would not discuss it any further. Without the blessing of the Fuhrer, Himmler continued with the project of raising a Guerrilla army of Nazi die hards, ranging from citizens loyal to the Reich, and from across the armed forces. Their role would be to allow the enemy to occupy Germany, and then cause trouble from within. Killing enemy soldiers not mindful of their personal security. Murdering any German citizens seen to collaborate with the invaders. The code name that was given to this band of brigands was 'Werewolf'.

Josef Goebbels also came on side with the idea, and promoted 'Radio Werewolf', a pirate radio broadcast designed to win over the German public, and also instruct them on how to use the standard infantry weapons of the German Army. These broadcasts enjoyed a limited element of success, when citizens would rise up against the invaders, ambushing couriers or outriders transiting between headquarters, disrupting rail links of enemy supply. There was certain 'Werewolf' success in the assassination of newly elected officials of German towns and cities. Puppet politicians put in place by the occupying forces.

Their actions throughout Germany were more of a nuisance than a real sting in the side of the occupying forces. The British were subject to some 'Werewolf' activity in the early years of occupation, but the Americans and the Russians took the brunt of their actions up to the mid 1950s'.

The 'Werewolves' knew that the Russians were not shy in carrying out reprisals for attacks on their supply convoys, and they in turn would serve nothing more than just to swell the 'Werewolf' ranks in the Soviet zone. For the majority, the uprising never really materialised, and the 'Werewolves' activities went from the traditional violent acts to more passive acts of non-compliance. Not co operating with new laws and guidelines put in place by the occupiers served to frustrate the Allies for a while, but before long, even those acts became weary, and those who opposed the occupation merely fell in line with the rest of Germany.

As the devils' advocate, regardless of who started the war. If your country was invaded, what would you do?
Surrender? Collaborate? Or resist?

Rob Lofthouse.

# PROLOGUE

"American recce, 800 metres!"

My stomach turned over, and a cold sweat began to over whelm me, Marco wasn't fairing much better. Max could see this and he took us both by the arms and pushed us to the back of the room.

"It's okay boys, let them get real close, they are less effective up close, trust me on this, just relax! You know how to use your weapons, so there is no problem, agreed?"

We nodded, this Russia and Normandy veteran knew how this would play out, all we had to do was our duty for Germany, and make sure every shot counted.

"Stay below the window, and prepare your weapons, and wait for my orders, whatever you hear in the street, do not look out until I say so, do you understand?" With that he moved into the next room to calm Karl and Bruno, who were getting just as agitated as us. We dragged all our weapons and equipment to the rear of the room and sat on the bed. Despite my trembling hands, I managed to prepare my Panzerfaust for action, and I then helped Marco with his. There was an extra two rockets each in the room, and it felt wise to prepare them also, since there was every chance of more than one target to shoot at below us, and it gave our hands something to do other than shake. I took hold of my rifle and ensured the magazine was fitted properly and I had easy access to my additional magazines, because what tends to accompany Tanks? Infantry.

Marco and I were soon set to go, and with our strict orders to not look out of the window, there was really nothing else left to do than just sit on the bed and wait for the time to fight. I sat quietly, trying to tune in with all that was going on outside. Outside I heard the odd clatter of boots on the road, probably where some of our guys were setting up for the ambush. I could hear the constant drum of engine noise, and the occasional revving of engines some distance away, but yet to establish which side was making the noise.

"American armour, 800 metres, recce vehicles, 600 metres", came the cry from somewhere downstairs. My stomach tightened all the more. Very shortly, all hell was going to let loose, I started to shiver with what could only be described as pre-match nerves. I looked at Marco, he looked just as terrified as me, and he broke into a broad grin, as his eyes started to well up, tears streaking down his face. It was okay to cry, I wasn't going to ridicule him for that, and I was only just holding it in myself.
Max burst into the room, which scared the shit out of the pair of us, he slid to his knees full of excitement.

"The Americans are marching in column, not battle formation, this is just too easy"

With that he then scrambled into the next room to inform the boys of this apparent amazing news. Marco and I just looked at each other and shook our heads. Max, a veteran of such situations as the one I found myself in right now, clearly had the experience to see the good in every situation, the Americans marching in column, by the sounds of things meant they were just bumbling along without a care in the world and would soon be in Paderborn in time for coffee and doughnuts. This revelation all of a sudden filled my chest with pride and my fears suddenly evaporated away. They will not be in Paderborn tonight, or any night, because we were going to stop them here, today!

"Recce, 300 metres", came the update from below. We were now below the window on our haunches ready to spring up for action. My hands were sweating like mad, and yet my mouth was bone dry. I cradled my first panzerfaust in my hands, and running through my mind the firing drills taught just the other day on the Senne. If the weapon was to fail and not fire, I would throw it at the nearest tank, in the vain hope it would launch, and cause some damage to the target as I grabbed my second one. I put the weapon carefully on the floor, worried the enemy recce crew would hear it over their engine noise, which was just ridiculous, but I was so hyped up at this stage, I would hear a mouse fart in a hurricane. I wiped my slippery hands over my thighs in an attempt to dry them. They were as dry as they were going to be and as I picked up the rocket once more, I could hear the drone of vehicles in the street as they slowly crept past below our window.

This was it surely, Max, give the command.

I flicked my eyes to Marco, he was breathing heavily, and blinking like he had something in both eyes, I'm pretty sure above the din of engines below us, I could hear his heart beating, or could it have been mine?

The drone was starting to fade, since the recce vehicles were being allowed through in order for us to get the main prize, the tanks. Heavier engines could now be heard very close to our window, they slowly grew louder and the building started to vibrate, ornaments in our room stated to dance across their respective surfaces, some clattering to the ground. The engine noise was building up to a climax, and the din was horrendous as what could be the first tank to pass under our fire position.

"FIRE" roared Max.

# PART ONE
## 1.

Never did I think that at eighteen years old, I would be fighting a war on the outskirts of my own home town.

Our mission was to destroy the Americans at Borchen, six kilometres south of Paderborn. The Americans are literally just a few kilometres away, and I would be a liar if I didn't admit I was scared. This time yesterday, we were conducting anti-armour ambush training in Senne, just north of the city. Our instructors were literally in the middle of a lesson with us, when we got the call to pack up our gear and march to Borchen. The direct route was out of the question, we marched through Marienloh, Nuenbeken, Dahl, and we would get into Borchen in the early hours. We passed through Nuenbeken in the middle of the night, and it was just as well we didn't go direct through Paderborn.

The British bombers pounded the rail yards in the centre of the city like you wouldn't believe. With bombs so powerful, we could feel the concussion of the raid on our bodies as we skirted our way around the outskirts.

I could only pray quietly to myself that mother would be okay, and Bad Lippspringe would be spared. Bad Lip lay on the north east outskirts of the city, and I would like to think there was nothing of real value that would attract the attention of the bombers. But who knew how accurate their bombing was, stranger things have happened. If they had come to learn of our column moving through the darkness to engage the Americans, it would have not end well for us.

Marching on the road was out of the question, we could only march in the drainage ditches that ran alongside, they were a mixture of waterlogged horseshit and mud. Slogging through the thick sludge was exhausting, and the whole experience was made all the more amusing and grim in equal measure when someone in the column slipped and ended up on their knees in it. I made it my mission that night to stay on my feet in the ditches, since I was not in the mood to bathe in horse crap.

Tanks rumble passed our column, in small groups throughout the march. They were a mixed bag of our heavier beasts, Panthers with their 76mm gun, along with the tank destroyer variant with its fixed turret, the Jagdpanther, capable of knocking out most variants of Sherman the British and Americans cared to throw at us, not to mention what the Russians had in vast numbers. Mixed in with the Panther class, were a few Tigers and their 88mm guns. They grinded passed flicking mud and crap all over us infantry peasants in the ditches. Our instructors told us all about the Tiger and its reputation in Russia. The Russians would lose their nerve on the battlefield as soon as it became apparent that Tigers were in the area. This buoyed my confidence in those machines since I'm sure we would see the Americans off in next to no time with their devastating firepower.

We rested briefly on the route, to allow the stragglers to catch up with their heavy loads. The machine gunners were not enjoying the night's effort since they carried pretty much the full load, gun, tripod, sight and as much belt link ammunition they could carry. The remainder of our company didn't fare much better. We were all loaded down with anything that we could use to slow the Americans down. As we trudged off the Senne towards Marienloh, we passed behind a series of trucks that were filled to the point of spill with panzerfausts. These crude yet effective rockets could knock out a Sherman no problems at all. It was a basic thin tube design, with a very crude sight and firing mechanism. The warhead itself was a large bulbous projectile that had enough explosive power to penetrate any vehicle the Americans threw at us. The skill required to use these rockets was not so much in your marksmanship, it was simply having the balls, not to mention nerve and allow the tank to get real bloody close, maybe one hundred metres or less. Our instructors, who were now our battle commanders constantly drummed it home to us that we must not panic when tanks are close. They are less dangerous the closer they are, since they are nothing more than a large metal box with scared people inside. Allow them to stand off at distance, exploiting their weapons sights and firepower was a nightmare for any infantry trying to knock them out, Russia taught our instructors these revelations.

As we crossed farmland just short of coming down into Dahl, over our right shoulder we could see Paderborn as a bright glow. The bombers had hit her hard, and continued to do so. The city centre was nothing more than an inferno, so bright it lit up the surrounding streets and large buildings, whatever one's appeared to remain standing. I looked further round to my right, in the general direction of Bad Lip, and that appeared to remain hidden in the darkness, which suited me just fine. My shoulders ached with my equipment. My standard issue helmet, with its grey and green fleck tarn helmet cover was wedged firmly on my head; sweat was slowly running down my temples and gathering under my chin strap. My field grey tunic was hidden under my fleck tarn smock, which was just a large, thin lightweight jacket. My field grey trousers were tucked into my leather jack boots, and in no fear of falling down due to my braces that had the trouser wedged right up the crack of my arse, I just couldn't be bothered to deal with it at this time. My fighting gear consisted of my leather yoke and belt; the yoke formed a y-shape between the shoulder blades and went over the shoulders to help hold the weight of your gear. On my belt, I had a pouch to hold my rifle magazines, a water bottle, my gas mask and canister, and my mini shovel, so when we got to our new positions, if needs be we could dig in.

As for weapons, I was sporting the STG44, an assault rifle, which I had slung across my right side, a Panzerfaust in my left hand, and squeezed down the front of my leather belt, two stick grenades. I also had the delight of carrying a tin of belt ammunition for the machine gunners, who had to feed the hungry appetite of their MG42's, a terrific weapon, I used it on the ranges a short while ago, and I found it to be very effective. My load was cutting into my shoulders, but there was no room to complain since everyone else in the column, including our instructors were in the same boat.

We began to descend down towards Dahl and skirt around to the right on what would be the last stretch into Borchen. The bombing of Paderborn had all but finished, the drone of the bombers was fading away, since they had done what they had come to do. Every now and again you could hear muffled explosions as fuel and other combustibles went up in flames. My mind started to wander. What have I got myself into here? I was the youngest of three boys. I was literally just at the tail end of my training in Senne, when we get orders for Borchen. My eldest brother, Willi, was killed in France last year, and Manfred, the middle sibling, has not been in touch for some time now. Last I heard, he was in Russia, I hoped he was okay. I just wish he would at least let mother know all is well. It is no secret that the Russians don't take SS prisoners, since we are the best German soldiers on the battlefield, and are therefore dangerous. I just want Manfred to write to mother and put her at ease.

Before long, Borchen came into view, and we slowly made our way down into the broad ravine that Borchen sits in. We crossed the river via the road bridge and as we made our way up out the other side we were ushered of to the left side of the road into a field and told to rest. This was a very welcome command, and I slumped against the bank that marked the edge of the road. Straight away the feeling in my shoulders felt like a gift from the gods. I adjusted myself so I could get to my water bottle, but it was not as easy as I had hoped. The lad in front of me on the march, Marco, leaned over and helped me get to my water.

'Thank you my friend.'

Marco nodded, 'no problem.'

Marco shared the same barracks as me in Senne, and could not have been much older than me. He was from Minden, I knew that much, but other than that, we didn't have much to do with each other. We both just sat there, leaning against the bank looking out over someone's farmland, waiting for our next move. I peered left and right, and all down the column, there was a mixed bag of activity. Sleeping, nose-picking, ball scratching, smoking, farting. As far as I was concerned, the SS was not known for its charm, how some of this lot ever landed a girlfriend was a mystery to me. Word came down the line for commanders to move up to the front of our column. At various points along the bank, individuals struggled to their feet, and trudged their way up to the front of the column. The perks of being in charge I suppose. I took the opportunity to remove my helmet, and get some air to my sweaty brow. A chill swept through me rather quickly as my sweaty body began to dry out; this however did not prevent my heavy eyelids from starting to close. I would savour this brief respite, since I'm sure it would be some time before the occasion presented itself again.

After a while, I'm not too sure how long since I had drifted off, our commanders came back down the line to join us. Max, our commander knelt down in front of me and called for our undivided attention.

'Right my lads listen up.'

His 'guys' consisted of me and about eight others, who were sat left and right.

'We have just sited where we will be taking up positions.'

He paused to allow this to sink in.

'The Americans made a huge land grab yesterday, since them lazy Army bastards did nothing to slow them down. Lead American elements will knocking on our door by mid morning tomorrow at the latest. Our job is to hit them hard, and the move back to the stone quarry which will be our secondary position. This will give us some breathing space, as the Americans will then be more cautious.'

We looked at each other; it suddenly dawned on us that this was going to be for real.

'Hey, listen you lot. We need to stop the Americans here tomorrow. We cannot allow them Paderborn, if they take Paderborn, they then have an open road to Berlin, do you understand?'
We nodded, this was real. He continued.

'The Americans hate SS, if they capture you, and don't shoot you on the spot, they will hand you over to the Russians, and those cowboys will use your mothers and sisters as whores.'

My stomach turned over.

'Get ready to move; as we move up to our positions, I will point out the stone quarry to you. When you hear the order to "break clean", you are to make your way there with your equipment and any wounded, is that clear?'

With that, we struggled to our feet. I adjusted myself, so my gear was somewhat more comfortable, and joined our column on the road. What appeared as somewhat of a surprise was the large numbers of civilians coming out of their houses and making their way passed us towards the bridge. The old and young alike, carrying literally what they could stuff into a suitcase, the mothers with their baby carriages and whatever they could fit underneath them. One old man in particular was speaking rather loudly about the fact that it was left to children to hold back the Americans, and the fighting men were lost in Russia. One of our instructors told him to be silent and go away. The old man continued to mumble about children having to fight the Americans, not real men. I thought the old fool was just babbling away, I was young, let it be said, but I wasn't going to let the Americans have my hometown, not while I had the means to do so. I peered down at my panzerfaust, I had good intentions planned with this, and that was a burning American tank, by my hand.

## 2.

We began to move off up the hill, it wasn't long before those up front pointed to the right and indicated the stone quarry. I had a good long look at it, since I had every intention of seeing it again. We kept to the left side of the road, behind us there was commotion as a platoon of four Panthers slowly made their way across the bridge, their commanders waving the civilians out of the way. Once across the bridge they pulled off the road and parked up. By the looks of things we would have some tank support when the Americans turned up; this made me feel a little better. As we began to make our way between the houses, Max told our squad to stay put while he looked around the house assigned to us, to determine where we were going to fight from. It wasn't long before he returned and beckoned us forward. He forced open the large wooden cellar doors and we followed him down into the darkness.

Once in, and we got used to the low light conditions, Max told us this is where his reserve was going to be. He didn't want all his fighting power leaning out of windows, since this would just be too good a target for American tanks to ignore. Besides the cellar, the house we occupied had two additional floors, the ground floor, plus the first floor. Max only wanted us to occupy the road side of the house, since the plan was to knock out as many vehicles in one shock attack and withdraw to the quarry. Machine gunners were to occupy the ground floor, and those with panzerfaust on the first floor, the riflemen were to act as reserve in the basement. The method to the madness was for the panzerfaust teams to hit the vehicles from above, which is a weak point on any vehicle, and the machine gunners were to deal with the crews bailing out. The riflemen would plug the gaps should any of the squad above be killed or wounded. The reserve would also act as stretcher bearers and get the casualties into the cellar, ready for the break clean. This was Max's advice from the Russian school of close combat.

Max took me, Marco, and two other guys, Bruno and Karl to the top floor and paired us up respectively. Bruno and Karl were put into what appeared to be the room where children normally slept, Marco and me in the master bedroom, both of which looked over the main road that flowed through Borchen. One room at a time, Max called us to our respective window, and explained what he wanted to happen.

'They will probably send their shitty little Recce vehicles through first, just to check the way ahead, whatever you do, don't be seen by these guys, or the game is up, clear?'

We both nodded, Max knew his stuff, he had done a lot of time in both Russia and Normandy, and so we gave him our undivided attention.

'Do not be tempted to take on the recce vehicles, the boys below you will take care of them. You are to take on the tanks, nothing else. Any of their infantry get into the house, stay quite, only fire at them if they come into the room, understand?'

We nodded.

'Remember, only fire on the tanks when I say so not before, hold your nerve, and when I say so, give them hell.'

Marco and I both grinned at each other, not too sure at this stage whether it was excitement or just nerves.

Marco made an observation; 'the road goes out of sight only about 50 metres away.'

Max nodded;' indeed it does young Marco, you want the tanks committed to your killing area, and you not committed to theirs. You are shooting down at them; therefore they cannot elevate high enough to shoot you.'

All becomes clear now.

Max continued; 'remember guys, tanks only, aim just below where the turret meets the body, as soon as the rocket is on its way, get away from the bloody window, or else you wont be around long enough to admire your handy work. Prepare the next Faust at the back of the room then quickly step forward and engage the next vehicle, okay?'

Marco and I were content. Max added more to his instruction,

'Get some rest, stay away from the windows until I say. I'm going to brief up the rest of the guys, and then the reserve guys are going to prepare whatever food is left in the house for us.'

With that, Max made his way downstairs, to put the finishing touches to his plan. I didn't take my belt kit off, but all my ammunition, rifle and grenades were laid on the floor underneath our window, along with my helmet. It would be getting light soon, and the Americans could not be too far away.
Marco and I took the opportunity to lay on the master bed, and just rest our eyes. Sleep would not come; too much was going through my head. Mother, Willi, Manfred, impending combat, the war, fear of capture, fear of dying, what have you got yourself into here Erik?

The room was warm and cosy, which made me doze to the point of which my own snoring would wake me up. I felt a pang of guilt knowing that the family that lived here all but a short time ago had to flee since we chose to stop the Americans in their very street. I could detect a faint aroma of soap and perfume, and what could only be described as that smell you have in a room where people have been sleeping. I wondered if the family and their children would have somewhere safe and warm to sleep tonight, with friends or extended family. I didn't want to be fighting in pretty much my own neighbourhood, all through my training, and even earlier in the Hitler Jugend, I had visions of slaying the Russians on the eastern front far away from our women and children. The last real news we had received from the east was that we were holding the Russians at bay far from German borders, which gave us all that sense of security. Here in the west, we had to fight just as hard to keep the British and Americans from exploiting our mothers and sisters, as all our men folk would be handed over to the Russians as slaves. How long would this all last? Germany was a wounded animal, no two ways about it, but we couldn't allow our nation to be conquered by the Russians in the east, or the British and Americans in the west.

The clatter of tank tracks and the roar of engines made me panic and sit bolt upright on the bed. Marco sat up, but not for long as he lost his perch and fell to the side causing the bedside table and lamp to then crash to the ground with a clatter. I sat there, as I tried to get a feel for where the tank noise was coming from. Heavy boots could be heard on the steps and were near the top. All my weapons were on the other side of the room, underneath the window sill. Had we all slept through the American advance? Was there American infantry in the house? A dark figure walked into the room, it was Max.

'What are you pair of clowns doing?'

Relief washed over me, as Marco clambered to his feet and redressed the side table. Max walked over to the bed and sat on the end of it, in his hands was a piece of paper with some pencil markings, he beckoned us over. It became apparent rather quickly that he had made a sketch of the town and our positions. Max began to explain the sketch.

'Here's the town, here's us, and the direction the Americans are expected to come from.' He indicted all these points with a small pencil.

'The engines you can hear are those Panthers that crossed the bridge just behind us, they are split into pairs and will be set rear left and right of us near the river, the aim of which is to deal with any American armour or Infantry movement around the sides of our group of house here. They are under strict instructions not to fire at any of the buildings due to where friendly forces are located. They will only take on Infantry that are outside, any of which get into the houses we will have to take care of, understand?'

We both nodded; satisfied he had put us in the picture. Max looked up and noticed we had closed the windows.

'Keep the windows open, I don't want any fucking around with trying to get shutters open, since that will just draw fire very quickly, so get it sorted.'

We did as he instructed, and as he stood to leave the room, shouting could be heard from downstairs.

'American Recce, 800 metres!'

My stomach turned over, and a cold sweat began to over whelm me, Marco wasn't fairing much better. Max could see this and he took us both by the arms and pushed us to the back of the room.

'It's okay boys, let them get real close, they are less effective up close, trust me on this, just relax! You know how to use your weapons, so there is no problem, agreed?'

We nodded, this Russia and Normandy veteran knew how this would play out, all we had to do was our duty for Germany, and make sure every shot counted.

'Stay below the window, and prepare your weapons, and wait for my orders, whatever you hear in the street, do not look out until I say so, do you understand?' With that he moved into the next room to calm Karl and Bruno, who were getting just as agitated as us. We dragged all our weapons and equipment to the rear of the room and sat on the bed. Despite my trembling hands, I managed to prepare my Panzerfaust for action, and I then helped Marco with his. There was an extra two rockets each in the room, and it felt wise to prepare them also, since there was every chance of more than one target to shoot at below us, and it gave our hands something to do other than shake. I took hold of my rifle and ensured the magazine was fitted properly and I had easy access to my additional magazines, because what tends to accompany Tanks? Infantry.

Marco and I were soon set to go, and with our strict orders to not look out of the window, there was really nothing else left to do than just sit on the bed and wait for the time to fight. I sat quietly, trying to tune in with all that was going on outside. Outside I heard the odd clatter of boots on the road, probably where some of our guys were setting up for the ambush. I could here the constant drum of engine noise, and the occasional revving of engines some distance away, but yet to establish which side was making the noise.

'American armour, 800 metres, Recce vehicles, 600 metres', came the cry from somewhere downstairs. My stomach tightened all the more. Very shortly, all hell was going to let loose, I started to shiver with what could only be described as pre-match nerves. I looked at Marco, he looked just as terrified as me, he broke into a broad grin, as his eyes started to well up, tears streaking down his face. It was okay to cry, I wasn't going to ridicule him for that, and I was only just holding it in myself.

Max burst into the room, which scared the shit out of the pair of us, he slid to his knees full of excitement.

'The Americans are marching in column, not battle formation, this is just too easy.'

With that he then scrambled into the next room to inform the boys of this apparent amazing news. Marco and I just looked at each other and shook our heads. Max, a veteran of such situations as the one I found myself in right now, clearly had the experience to see the good in every situation, the Americans marching in column, by the sounds of things meant they were just bumbling along without a care in the world and would soon be in Paderborn in time for coffee and doughnuts. This revelation all of a sudden filled my chest with pride and my fears suddenly evaporated away. They will not be in Paderborn tonight, or any night, because we were going to stop them here, today!

'Recce, 300 metres', came the update from below. We were now below the window on our haunches ready to spring up for action. My hands were sweating like mad, and yet my mouth was bone dry. I cradled my first panzerfaust in my hands, and running through my mind the firing drills taught just the other day on the Senne. If the weapon was to fail and not fire, I would throw it at the nearest tank, in the vain hope it would launch, and cause some damage to the target as I grabbed my second one. I put the weapon carefully on the floor, worried the enemy recce crew would hear it over their engine noise, which was just ridiculous, but I was so hyped up at this stage, I would hear a mouse fart in a hurricane. I wiped my slippery hands over my thighs in an attempt to dry them. They were as dry as they were going to be and as I picked up the rocket once more, I could hear the drone of vehicles in the street as they slowly crept past below our window.

This was it surely, Max, give the command.

I flicked my eyes to Marco, he was breathing heavily, and blinking like he had something in both eyes, I'm pretty sure above the din of engines below us, I could hear his heart beating, or could it have been mine?

The drone was starting to fade, since the recce vehicles were being allowed through in order for us to get the main prize, the tanks. Heavier engines could now be heard very close to our window, they slowly grew louder and the building started to vibrate, ornaments in our room stated to dance across their respective surfaces, some clattering to the ground. The engine noise was building up to a climax, and the din was horrendous as what could be the first tank to pass under our fire position.

# 3.

"FIRE" roared Max.

I sprung up like a ferret and before me was the most surreal scene I could ever of imagined.

Beneath us was what could only be described as a traffic jam. Green and brown armoured vehicles crammed into such a confined space that was the road through Borchen. We didn't need to aim, just point the rocket at the solid, smelly, clattering mass beneath us. I flipped the Faust onto my right shoulder and pointed at the second pair of tanks just low left of our window, the first two were already easy prey for the team in the house to our right. I squeezed the firing lever and there was a deafening roar as my rocket streaked away and smashed into my target in a flurry of sparks. I dropped to the floor and scrambled to the rear of the room for my next rocket. Marco was right behind me scrambling frantically for his next one. I picked mine up and gave myself a second to compose myself, all the tension of the last hour was gone, and my mind clear of all reservation and doubt. I had just been baptized into the exclusive club that is combat. As I stood to launch myself at the window once again, a loud vibrating drum of MG42 could be heard followed instantly by high pitched drum of bullets striking steel. I stepped forward to the window, my first tank was billowing smoke, but no flames were visible. Its crew lay sprawled over the front and side of the smouldering hulk, the boys downstairs had dealt with them. I looked left and the tanks were trying to reverse, but tanks that were smouldering behind them prevented them from escaping. I took the care to aim at one that was trying to turn left between the houses opposite us. As I fired, the tank was just engulfed in numerous showers of sparks, as it was smashed by several rockets at once. It stopped dead, smoke billowing from its back engine decks. It was instantly sprayed in machine gun bullets, so the crew could not bail out. It looked like a huge beast that had kicked a hornet's nest. The crew never emerged.

I scrambled to the rear of the bedroom once again, cursing myself for getting caught up in the spectating that could very easily have killed me. Marco stepped forward and fired his rocket. He scampered over to me and we both took hold of our third rocket, as we now had the taste for tank killing.

"American infantry, in the house!"

My blood ran cold instantly, as the dull thud of grenades exploding could be heard in our cellar. The concussion from the grenades exploding caused the floorboards beneath our feet to crack and creak. The chattering of sub machine guns, screaming, shouting, more grenade thuds. Marco grabbed my arm,

"Remember what Max said; stay quite until they come into our room." I'm glad he remembered, it seemed so long ago.

The chaos of downstairs subsided, and all around our position, we heard different voices shouting.

"Break clean, break clean!"

Marco and I just looked at each other, waiting for the familiar voice of Max, our leader.
"Break clean, you fucking idiots!" Max roared up the stairs, which despite the insult made Marco and I chuckle with relief. Ensuring we had all but the used rocket tubes with us, we made our way quickly out of the room onto the landing, as I got to the top of the stairs, I was hit side on by a solid mass that sent me crashing against the wall and then clattering down the stairs with this greenish grey mass on top of me. I ended up in a heap at the bottom of the stairs.

Winded from the fall, I tried to curse out load, but the burning sensation in my chest did nothing but produce a hacking cough. The greenish grey mass turned out to be Bruno, the fucking oaf! Max stood over us, MG42 in one hand, rifle in the other shaking his head.

"Germanys finest!" he then turned and ran out into the street. I untangled myself from Bruno and then noticed the scene before me. Two fleck tarn bodies were slumped in a crumpled heap on the floor below the window frame. Mixed in with them was the olive green, muddy frame of what could only be an American. Flecks of blood decorated the wall they were leant against. The room reeked of cordite, and the copper tang of fresh blood, clear evidence of close combat. The dull thud of an explosion in another building snapped me out of my trance, and we made off after Max. It was a similar story in the street, let me tell you. The tanks were smouldering heavily, their engines still running, the heavy pungent smell of gasoline hung in the air. Dead tank crews were hanging out of their hatches, some in a crumpled, smouldering heap on the road. Some of the wounded crew members lay groaning in the street, some may even have played dead, so not to attract more gunfire. The four of us made off after Max, our heads on swivels as we tried to locate our other squad members, and also checking American infantry were not right behind us. We ran mob handed down the road towards the quarry, which would be our next defence line, since the Americans I'm sure were not going to let us get away with this ambush.

Just short of the quarry entrance, were the recce vehicles. Twisted, smouldering wrecks, their crews slumped in their sitting positions, riddled with bullets, faces smashed and caved in like eggs from the impact of various projectiles, some lying by the roadside, no doubt in an attempt to get away from their smashed vehicles and comrades, their blood pooling beneath them and slowly trickling down the kerbside towards the bridge.

As we entered the mouth of the quarry, there was sheer calamity before me. Wounded sat at the side of the track, being dressed in bandages by the medics clucking around them, Officers and NCOs' pushing and shoving their shell-shocked men into fighting positions, other Officers consulting maps and pointing out towards the lip of the quarry. Max pointed at a patch of ground where he wanted us to sit tight, placing the MG42 down at our feet.

"Wait here while I find out where these clowns want us."

He made his way into the melee of wounded and those still fit to fight. Marco and I slumped against the quarry wall, just to catch our breath. I took greedy gulps from my water bottle and nearly ended up wearing most of it, when the Panthers by the riverbank started firing. The Americans must be trying to push on. Max came jogging back over.

"Grab your shit, we are not staying here, the Americans will fuck us up in here, we are moving back towards the river, right now."

I scrambled to my feet and took up the MG42. To make things abit easier for me, Marco took my rifle and one remaining Panzerfaust. I stuck the '42 on my shoulder and rearranged the belt of ammunition so it wasn't twisted, and I could fight quickly if need be. Max then led us out of the quarry into the roadside ditch that led down towards the bridge. The Panthers were still taking on whatever they were shooting at. The other two positioned above the quarry were now joining in too. As I carefully, but rather quickly scampered after Max down the ditch, I noticed the Panthers by the bridge rocking backwards on their sprockets and tracks in a flurry of sparks as they took the punishment of the American armour trying to knock them out. The Panthers would then reply in kind, which was comforting, since they were keeping the Americans busy amongst the buildings to our rear. As we drew near the first span of

the small crossing, the Panther crews leaped out of their tanks and scrambled over towards us and joined us in the ditch.
"Out of fuel, cant move", said one of the grubby, sweaty panzer crewmen.

Max leaned towards Marco, taking my rifle from him, and threw it at the crewman,

"Welcome to the Infantry, follow me!"

Their faces were a picture, which caused Marco and me to chuckle, no more languishing in a tank, now in the muddy ditch with the rest of us.

We all scrambled down to the river bank, it was rather shallow, the riverbed clearly visible. Without ceremony Max jumped in and waded across, with us blundering through after him, the water was cold, and being knee deep, it poured into our boots with no effort, great. On the far bank, we quickly emptied our boots, and made our way through the first row of two story buildings and out-houses. The gardens were separated but two-strand fences and chicken coops were dotted about the place. Chickens clucked loudly in their dwellings as we sought to get out of the light drizzle that had begun to coat us. Some troops were breaking into the first of the buildings, but Max very quickly reprimanded them.

"Get out of there you fucking idiots, they will just stand off and shoot the shit out of the bloody building, occupy the next row."

They sheepishly looked at each other, until almost at once, the penny dropped. With new found energy, they dashed out of the gardens and forced their way into the house directly behind it. This was a good move; once again Russia had taught us to not occupy the outer ring of buildings, since the Russians would just sit back and let the tanks shoot up all the houses. By occupying the second row, the tanks and infantry had to come in closer which then put them on our terms, and evened the odds. As we got to the road we skirted left and Max made a bee line for the first house we encountered on the right side. He led us around the back, and with the gentle persuasion of a hard kick, the kitchen door gave way. We then occupied the house with ourselves and our newly recruited Panzer crews. Max quickly put us to task.

"Faust men upstairs, Erik you stay down here with me, you lot sit tight in the kitchen." The men he addressed as "you lot" being the panzer crews. "I will put you guys where I want you when it all gets crazy around here, understand!"

They nodded, their expressions gave away the fact they were so out of their comfort zone. But then again, who the fuck was comfortable about this whole situation anyway? We went about our business, remembering what Max had drummed into us during the earlier ambush. I made my way into what was the communal room, and placed the '42 below the main window which looked out onto the road, but a house opposite prevented me from seeing the river and large field beyond which lay the quarry. Even the cluster of buildings we occupied earlier was out of sight. I took comfort in this; it would mean the Americans couldn't see this building properly. I ensured the shutters and windows were open, as before, and I then moved to the back of the room and sat in the comfortable chair. I removed my helmet, placing it on my right knee, and surveyed the room. Everything looked in its right place, no sign of people rushing to pack their possessions, all very tidy and orderly. The large shrank unit along the left wall was adorned in lovely framed family pictures. Once again, there was evidence of a young family living here. Numerous pictures of babies and toddlers were placed all over the room. I pondered the fate of this family, total strangers to me, but I wished them good health, and felt a pang of guilt, since I would shortly bring the war to this beautifully kept room, literally.

I could hear movement upstairs, probably Max siting the guys' right where he wanted them. I heard boots on the stairs as someone came down and clatter into the kitchen at the back. Max then emerged with one of the black clad panzer crewmen. It was the guy Max had thrown my rifle at.

"Young Bobby here is going to fight this position with you, ok?" Max then disappeared, while Bobby found himself a place to sit. I leaned over and offered my hand.

"I'm Erik, nice to meet you Bobby; sorry the circumstances couldn't be more appealing"

Bobby grinned, and accepted my hand, "nice to meet you Erik, let's hope we can bore our grandchildren with this meeting, don't you agree?"

I noticed Bobby wasn't exactly as young as Max had claimed. He was certainly older than I; the long scar on his left cheek indicated either recent action in the service of the Fuhrer, or a tough
Childhood. We both sat back in our chairs, I felt at a loss with regards to what we could talk about, so I played it cool, and took interest in my helmet cover. Bobby broke the ice.

"Are you from around here Erik?"

"Yeah, Bad Lippspringe, just north of Paderborn. You?"

"Frankfurt" Bobby replied, "On the Oder"

I winced, "any news from there?"

Bobby just looked down into his own lap, "the Russians are there, that's all I know."

# 4.

It was clear all was not well in the east, if the Russians were in Bobby's hometown, then they were definitely in Germany, not good at all. I just hoped that our guys over there could keep them from getting any further into our country. Those lazy Army bastards as usual leave it to the SS to hold the line and smash the Russians, but we can't be in two places at once. What have you got yourself into here Erik?

Out in the street, but out of sight to the right I could hear the rumbling groan of what I could only guess was an armoured vehicle. The grind of transmission, and the rumbling got louder, causing the house to shudder, the ornaments in the room danced slightly. Max came into the room, with his trusty piece of paper once again. He sat on the right arm of my chair. Pencil poised at his hasty sketch.

"Here's the quarry, the bridge and river, and this is how the houses sit in the street."

Bobby and I shuffled around to orientate ourselves to his sketch. Max continued.

"Next to us is a Jagdpanther, ready to go, we've got our guys sited in these houses here, here, and here. At the entrance to the road, next to the bridge, there are MG 42's that will take care of an Infantry crossing; the Jagdpanther plus a couple of 20mm flak guns further to the right will deal with an armour approach."

I'm not a tactician, but to me that didn't sound like much to stop the Americans.

"We've got a couple of guys in an observation position in the front row of houses that will drip feed information to us, should the Americans move out of the quarry. Same drill as before, when a tank is hit, you spray like a bastard, and be prepared for their Infantry, got it?"

I nodded, our panzer crewman wasn't quite as confident, clearly not in the comfort bubble of his Panther, and his facial expression gave the game away. Max placed his hand on Bobby's shoulder.

"You'll be fine, just do what Erik does, and don't get killed."

Great advice, if there ever was any. Bobby nodded, still not completely sold on the whole thing, but tough shit, this was what was happening, and so he'd better step up and help me hold this house.

Out in the direction of the quarry, I could hear the sound of engines revving and roaring, the echo of engine noise in a confined space could not be mistaken. No mention of the Americans appearing yet, if I was a betting man, they were getting their act together before taking another shot at the title. I ran through my mind what the Americans would have to do to get into a position to blast this house into rubble. They could probably just see the top of our roof once out of the quarry, but apart from reducing the house in front of us to rubble and get line of sight to us, they would have to get across the open field and near the river bank to get the angle required for a tank shot. They would have to dance with the Jagdpanther first, as well as the flak guns. I wasn't entirely convinced we had what was required to keep them in the quarry, but it's all we had, plus some of us in the houses for good measure.

I could hear commotion in the kitchen behind us. Rattling of pots and pans, running water, breaking of crockery, troops cursing, the usual calamity when troops are trying to be quiet. It wasn't long before I could smell the aroma of coffee, and what could only be described as vegetables being cooked. It suddenly dawned on me that I hadn't eaten since supper last night in Senne before we marched here. Max's promise of an early breakfast did not materialise since the Americans decided to turn up, how rude of them. I wasn't fussed by what was being cooked to be honest, since I didn't have to cook it, and to top it off, I was bloody hungry. Max leaned around the doorway.

"Take it in turns, get in here and get some food."

I looked at Bobby, "you eat first, and I will wait."

I made my way into the kitchen, and the room was in total disarray. They remaining panzer crewmen were now combat cooks, and must have used every pot and pan in the kitchen to prepare our food. On the large wooden table in the centre of the room were different pots and pans containing vegetables and potatoes. A large jug of coffee was perched on the end, and to be fair, it all smelt rather appealing.

"Not your mothers quality I'm afraid" one of the crewmen piped up "but better than a kick in the tits."

Fair point, I grabbed one of the small pots, and one of our chefs poured me a coffee, whilst shoving two forks into my free hand.

"Share with Bobby, plenty more coffee, if you want it."

Very nice. I scampered back into the room Bobby and I occupied, taking care not to pour the red hot coffee over my hand. Bobby pulled the two comfy chairs together and we balanced the pot and the cup of coffee on the adjoining arms of the chairs. We wanted to eat in comfort. We tucked greedily into the pot with our forks, taking no prisoners. We shovelled it in like pigs in the trough, our mothers would disapprove of our table manners, lets put it that way. The food was basic, but it certainly did the trick, before long, our bellies were full. We took our time over the coffee, savouring every sip. Tank fire not too far away almost made me drop the cup in my own lap. We carefully scrambled over to the window and peered out. No commotion outside, the lads keeping watch in the house opposite us didn't appear to be concerned, so who the hell was doing the shooting?

Max leaned into the room, "keep low, I'm going to find out what the fuss is about", and with that he scarpered out the back of the house.

It wasn't coming from the quarry, we knew that much. It echoed loudly towards us from the East. Did we have friendly forces in that direction? Ambush? Artillery? One thing that was certain, it was bloody constant.

"Those are our tanks firing" Bobby piped up, "Eighty-eights, probably Tigers."

"How can you tell?" I pushed.

"Sherman's give off a dull thud, listen"

Amid the din, I strained to hear of this so-called thud. I heard what could only be a single thud amid the loud recoiling echo of the eighty-eights. If I was judging it right, the Americans weren't firing as much as ours, I wasn't exactly sure. After a while in the waning light, the echoing tank fire began to reduce to the odd shot here and there. Max was back and stood in the doorway, summoning us into the kitchen. Bobby and I kept a low profile until we were clear of the window, and stood up comfortably in the kitchen. Marco, Karl and Bruno came down from their rooms and joined us with our panzer crewmen around the large wooden table. Max beckoned in a few more new faces from outside, introducing them as our Jagdpather crew who's vehicle continued to idle and throb next to the house, clearly what Max had to tell us was important. He called for us to quieten down.

"The Americans have tried to flank us by moving a large tank force through Hamborn, just down the road. What they didn't bank on was our anti-tank screen that just so happened to be sat in the wood line overlooking their route. What you heard earlier was our guys smashing them to a standstill, and therefore another bloody nose for the Americans."

The Jagd crew stifled a chuckle, and shook hands, clearly members of the same unit that ambushed the Americans. Max continued.

"It will be dark soon, but don't get comfortable, since all we've done once again is stir the hornets nest, and if any of you have met the Americans before, you know well enough they won't call it a day just because we've given them a good hiding, so don't get cocky."

"Americans!" came a loud shout from outside.

We scattered like bugs caught in torchlight back to our fighting positions. My stomach turning over with pre-match nerves. I wasn't ready, this wasn't good for me. I didn't want to fight in the dark. We got beneath our window frame and put our helmets on, and went to work ensuring our weapons were good to go. Palms slippery with sweat, not much I could do about that apart from wiping them on my thighs once again. I was ready to go, heart pounding in my ears, but ready. I peered out of the window, the light was fading, and it wouldn't be long before it was dark. I strained to hear approaching vehicles over the idling engine of the Jagdpanther sat by our window. Our sentries in front of us gave us what we needed.

"Armour, troop carriers, and walking Infantry, line abreast, 400 metres, more coming out of the quarry."

Shit, this place was going to get real busy soon. I heard the Jagd engine change tempo, and begin to creep forward, causing the house to vibrate. It came to a standstill just short of the right side of our sentry post, whose occupants were vacating at a crouching run, and making their way to our window. Without ceremony, they clambered through the window, and slumped on the floor in front of us.

"The Jagd has got some work to do," said one of them, "there is fucking loads of them."

Great, not what I want to hear.

They clambered to their feet, and scrambled out of the room, probably looking for their new fighting position. Max then scampered in at a crouch.

"Same drill as before boys, don't expose yourselves until I say. If they knew we were here, they would have smashed us with artillery by now, so keep away from the window. Let the Jagd do its stuff."

Without waiting for us to acknowledge, he was off upstairs. Bobby and I left our weapons under the window, and took refuge at the back of the room, behind the comfy chairs. Out in the fields to our front, I could hear the groaning and rattling of engines, the Americans were getting close. There was then, an almighty thud, and my world just became nothing more than a high pitched whine. The Jagdpanther was taking on the unseen enemy. As the whine faded, battle noise soon replaced it. I could make out; off to our right a rapid beat of a drum. The flak guns were now in the fight.

"Get ready!" roared Max. Bobby and I scrambled out from our little sanctuary, and got ourselves under the window, helmets on; weapons in hand, ready to fight. Getting the MG42 onto the window frame would be abit awkward, but not impossible. I peered up, to look at the Jagd, as it fired again, the soundtrack of whining returned with a vengeance. I continued to watch the tank as it fired round after round at an enemy I had yet to lay eyes on in this particular engagement. The house next to the tank suddenly burst with a muffled thud, showering the Jagd in bricks, roof tiles and glass. As my hearing returned, our house vibrated violently as the Jagd reversed away from the wrecked building, dragging with it, a lot of house debris. It pulled up level with our house and with a high pitched squeal of engine and transmission, turned sharply to the left.

One of its turret hatches creaked open and I saw one of its black clad crewman clamber out, quickly getting to work clearing the house debris off the top of his vehicle. I must have caught his attention, he stopped what he was doing and grinned at me and gave me a casual salute. He then went back to work clearing his vehicle of bricks and tiles. Something off to our left caught his attention; he scrabbled up to his open hatch and began screaming instructions into it. I was curious as to what the emergency was, as I peered out to our left, a mud smeared Sherman was visible through a gap between the houses on the other side of the road. My world then became nothing more than a piercing scream in my ears and a brilliant white flash.

As my vision swam back into focus, I could see Bobby lying on his side facing me, hands on his ears shaking his head. The high pitched whine still screamed in my ears. I propped myself up on my left side and pushed myself back towards the wall under the window frame. The house vibrated violently and constant, ornaments dancing off their perches, hitting the floor with a muffled thud. The vibrating eased off to a slight rumble. I saw Max crawl into the room, and begin talking to us. I couldn't understand the dull muffle. He rolled his eyes, and grabbed me by my smock, sitting me upright. The whine in my ears began to fade, making Max's dialogue all the more understandable.

"The Americans have fallen back!" he bellowed at me, "get your arses into the cellar, they will fuck us with artillery, make no mistake."

I slowly got to my feet, helping Max to get Bobby up and moving, since he was almost out of it. We got him to his feet, and ensuring we took our weapons with us, made our way into the kitchen that had a door underneath the stairs. This door led us down into a rather spacious cellar, which was rather bare, with the exceptions of a few empty wooden crates that contained straw. We set Bobby down, and checked out what was available to help us get comfortable. My hearing was as good as back, and I jumped when Max shouted up the cellar stairs.

"Get down in to the cellar, you fucking idiots!"

Instantly, I could hear the chaotic thudding of footsteps throughout the house as the boys clattered down to join us. Marco, upon seeing me still in one piece, gave me a wicked grin.

"That was pretty intense; the Jagd really gave the Americans what for."

As we slumped against the cellar wall, Max remained standing, hands on hips.

"Did those clowns fire next to our fucking house? I thought the whole place was about to collapse."

He must have been referring to the Jagd crew. Their barrel muzzle was right above our window when they took on that Sherman. They must have knocked it out; we are all alive to complain about them. Max picked up his weapons,

"Stay down here whilst I go and find out what is going on. If they are going to hit us with artillery, we need to just sit it out, they will be back."

With that, he climbed the stairs. The remainder of us just got comfortable, some shedding their gear, I chose to remain kitted up, but I did give in to temptation and remove my helmet. I could smell the welcoming aroma of tobacco. Some gulped greedily from their water bottles. I just slumped onto my side with my head on my right bicep in the vain attempt to rest. After a time, I began to doze; my snoring invited the occasional shove from Marco, who was also trying to sleep. Some of the guys chatted quietly, the subject remained that of home, the Russians, and Hitler's fucking war, anything that the boys wanted to get off their chests. We had no officers with us down here, so the lads chatted without restriction. SS or not, we knew it would take a miracle to change our current situation around. But if we just gave up, we risked being shot out of hand, or marched off to Siberia. The road to Berlin would be open, and that was just out of the question.

## 5.

Some of the lads started asking Bobby questions about fighting in
Russia. He was rather candid with his answers, explaining how
savage some of the engagements had been in his time out there. He
told us neither side took prisoners, and would literally smash each
other to oblivion. He told us he was part of the relief force sent to
help out at Stalingrad, but the weather, and the Russians were so
savage, that they couldn't get through. Up until now, we didn't
know the full story about this city known as Stalingrad. During my
time in training, I'd heard many stories about our brave fathers and
brothers holding Stalingrad to the last man and bullet. Bobby was
very quick to inform us that the Sixth Army was abandoned and
allowed to freeze and starve, which ever came first. He told us
about Kursk, this huge tank battle, where at one point our tanks
were literally crashing into theirs due to the dust. I took great
interest in these tales, since they were far more vivid than what we
had been told on the Senne. He then began to tell us about Jews
and the Einsatzgruppen...

"That's enough of that shit!" Max barked. I jumped out of my skin,
since we didn't hear him return.

Bobby stood up, "Just telling the boys about Russia."

"Don't be filling their heads with that nonsense", Max shook his
head, "I need you lot focused on the now, not war stories, is that
clear?"

We all nodded, Bobby included. Max motioned Bobby to relax, and
he too squatted down to talk at our level.

"The Americans have fallen back to the quarry. They will be back,
don't you worry about that. We need guys in the wrecked house
tonight, so we can give warning for another attack. I doubt we will

have any artillery issues tonight, since they would have done it by now. Return to your fighting positions."

We all clambered to our feet and we slowly shuffled up the cellar stairs. Bobby was in front of me, Max took him by the arm,

"No more stories about Russia, okay?"

Bobby nodded. We made our way up, back into our room. The room was intact, but covered in dust. A lot of the small ornaments were smashed all over the floor. The shutters on the window frame were almost shut. I carefully pushed them open; it was as good as dark now. I peered left and could make out the dark mass of the Sherman. Its turret was missing, flames licking around where it once sat, thick black smoke rose in a steady column from its back decks. I thought about its crew. Did the Jagdpanther kill them with the shell? Or did they bail out to fight another day? I wondered if the Americans reflected when they killed us, most probably. I doubt we would ever find out. Max came into the room.

"You two get yourselves into the damaged house. I will send your replacements over in a couple of hours, okay?"

We nodded, gathered up our kit and weapons and slowly eased ourselves over the window frame, carefully lowering ourselves to the ground and gingerly made our way across the road. As we approached the wrecked house, the Sherman let out an almighty pop, along with a shower of sparks, the ammunition or fuel must have finally cooked off. We made our way over the shattered bricks and tiles, trying to make as less noise as possible. The ground floor was pretty much intact, but upstairs was just a mess. We agreed to climb what was left of the stairs, and get a suitable perch so we could watch the quarry. Bobby scaled the wrecked stair case first, and then reached down to take the '42 off of me. I climbed with relative ease. Once on the landing, we carefully picked our way through the mess and found a decent spot. We were still on the landing but the room between us and the open field beyond the river had collapsed in on itself, allowing us a certain degree of cover. Out in the field was a scene that could only be described as carnage.

Black hulks of vehicles stood smouldering all over the place. The Jagdpanther crew had really earned their pay today. Some would crackle, and pop occasionally as their combustibles would succumb to heat and flame. It wasn't just tanks smouldering in the field, troop carriers were amongst them. Smaller pillars of smoke could be seen in the long grass around the vehicles, dead troops. I looked up at the sky, since our current position no longer had a roof, and it appeared to be slightly overcast. It wasn't particularly warm, but we only had to sit it out for a couple of hours. We sat ourselves down, with our backs against the banisters that kept us from falling downstairs. We cautiously leaned against it, fearing it would give way, but appeared sturdy enough. I didn't put the machine gun in any particular fire position; I just kept it next to my right thigh, as I sat cross legged on the landing. Bobby had what was once my rifle across his thighs. I was at a loss for what to talk about, so for a little while took comfort in the silence and just listened to the burning hulks popping and fizzing now and again. After a while, I thought I'd push my luck.

"Why does Max get touchy about Russia?"

Bobby sighed, looking down at his weapon.

"Can you ever imagine a place where you can literally murder people, and none of your comrades batter an eyelid?" He put to me. I shook my head. He continued.

"We will pay dearly for our actions in Russia, mark my words. My hometown is now in Russian hands. I dread what is going on there. I fear for my mother, my wife........my daughter."

Stories of wholesale rape where not uncommon amongst some of the stuff we had heard about Russia. But the Russians were now in Germany, with German women for the taking. He then continued with his unfinished story about the Jews and the Einsatzgruppen. Special squads of police and thugs in German uniforms, whose sole task was to round up Jewish civilians, and shoot them. Men, women, the old, the young, the pregnant, infants, no one was spared. Bobby took a deep breath.

"The Russians want revenge, they will not listen to the pleas of our people, they will have no mercy on us. We cannot guarantee the Americans, or the British will take much pity on us. We are in a world of shit of our own making. We will pay dearly as a nation, I assure you of that, young Erik."

I was horrified at what I had just heard. It had to be true. Why would Bobby say such things if it wasn't so? No wonder Max was touchy about the whole subject. Was he involved? Had he witnessed these actions? My stomach turned. We were in a bad position. We had to fight the Americans or risk something worse, falling into Russian hands. Would the Americans rape our women and girls? Would the British? The whole idea of it horrified me. What have you got yourself into here Erik?

"What should we do Bobby?" I pushed. He looked at me with glazed, watery eyes, and a half smile,

"Enjoy the war Erik, because the peace will be terrible."

Shit.

We sat in silence for a while, numbed by Bobby's confession. The flames on the knocked out vehicles had all but gone now, just a pillar of black smoke to mark their demise. I looked up towards the lip of the quarry. The moon had broken through the cloud, which made it all the more prominent. I wondered what the American sentries were talking about, Home? Women? Beer? No doubt they wanted this madness to end. With all the technology and weapons at our disposal, this fight still boiled down to two armies staring each other down across a muddy field. History has changed nothing in that sense.

Time passed slowly, until I heard the familiar crunch and scrape of boots picking their way through house debris behind us. I slowly got to my feet, which were partially numb, since I'd spent a lot of the last couple of hours sat cross legged. I peered down into the stair well, and as my vision improved, I could make out the profile of Karl and Bruno. Karl gave me a thumb's up, in which I returned the gesture. Space was abit tight up on the landing, so Bobby and I clambered down before the other lads took over. They didn't have to go upstairs, but it did give you a better view of the quarry and field beneath. Bobby led the way back to our previous position, crunching and cracking our way across the road. Bobby didn't go to our window; he led us around the left side of the house and into the kitchen at the rear. We put our weapons on the kitchen table, and Bobby got the little oil lamp on the table up to a soft light, illuminating the kitchen fixtures and the stove. I needed a piss, so as I stood at the back door, watering the garden, Bobby got the kettle on. I prepared the cups, coffee with a generous helping of sugar found in the cupboards. We sat at the table, all very civilised, waiting for the water to come to the boil. I looked at Bobby, who had his eyes closed, listening to the water begin to bubble. I had the million dollar question on my lips,

"Did you shoot any?"

He slowly turned his head, and opened his eyes.

"A long time ago, we were sat in a village in the middle of nowhere with engine trouble. Our unit had moved on telling us to catch up once repairs were complete. It was a beautiful hot day, and we had nothing better to do but sunbathe while waiting for the mechanics. I couldn't tell you who was Jewish or not, and to be perfectly honest, I didn't care. If there was a Jew who could fix my panzer in that village, I would have hired him, not shot him."

I let out a giggle; a soldier's humour was never far from the surface in any story, no matter how dark. Bobby continued,

"A small column of our trucks arrived; we thought it was the mechanics and spares. But it was full of soldiers and German Shepherds. They totally ignored us and moved straight into the buildings, dogs barking, and began turfing the families out. Everyone was scared, dogs snapping at the children, making them cry. These guys rounded up everyone and led them away towards the far end of the village. About an hour later, there was a lot of rifle and machine gun fire from that direction, followed shortly by our friends and theirs dogs, laughing and joking, smoking cigarettes, all very happy with themselves, bastards. They mounted up in their trucks, and drove off in the direction of our units moving forward."

I looked at my hands in my lap, "I'm sorry to have asked Bobby."

Bobby grinned, standing up to deal with the boiling kettle, "Its okay Erik, you are a bright kid, just take what you hear from now on with a pinch of salt, that's all the advice I can offer you."

We savoured our very sweet coffee in silence. I didn't ask anymore questions, not because I had no more to ask; I was scared of the answers I would hear. I made my mind up very quickly, fight the Americans, just do my duty, and no more. Our drinks finished, we made our way back into our room, and our comfy chairs. I stripped my gear off, and lowered myself slowly into my chair, it felt so nice and welcoming, in next to no time, Bobby was nudging me because of my snoring.

**6.**

"American armour in the street!"

I felt an almighty shove, I opened my eyes and as I began to focus, I saw Bobby below the window frame waving frantically at me.

"Get here Erik, Americans in the street."

I launched myself from the chair, straight on to the floor grabbing my weapons as I scrambled over to Bobby. The house was vibrating slightly, which indicated there was armour very close. It was as good as broad daylight outside, had our positions been caught napping, literally? Max crawled into the room,

"They just rumbled straight down the main road, across the bridge. They've turned into our street, get ready!"

I couldn't get the '42 into the window until the last moment, any sooner would be suicide. I could hear engines roaring as they continued to turn into our street. The now familiar rumbling of our building on its foundations was again present, but the ornaments in the room were well past their previous positions, all now scattered across the floor. Bobby and I just grimaced at each other, judging when to spring up and take the tanks on would be a one shot deal, too early would warn them, and too late could have another one of our positions in the street getting shot to pieces.

The streaking roar of Panzershrek down the street to our left made the decision for us. I sprung up on my haunches, to my horror looking straight into the eyes of the Sherman commander who happened to be looking through our window, his heavy machine gun pointing straight at me. He had me bang to rights; my MG42 still sat below the window frame on the floor. I pushed my feet backwards, allowing my frame to drop from sight and ensured I was spread thin on the floor waiting for the world to disintegrate around me.

As I hit the floor, I was winded with the force of my drop from view, there was a series of streaking roars, followed immediately by numerous thuds, sparks flickering through our window, all over us. A heavy hand grabbed the back of my smock,

"Get the fucking gun up now!" Bobby roared at me.

I quickly got to my knees, and clumsily got the gun up onto the window frame. The Sherman was sat where I had left it, smoke billowing from every hatch, and the engine decks. The American was slumped over his machine gun, minus his head. His blood smeared like a child's early painting around where the machine gun was mounted. The body flinched with bullet strikes as those above us were not taking any chances with its crew attempting to bail out. The billowing dark smoke made searching for targets difficult, since the tank took up most of our field of view. I had to quickly swivel the MG42 left and right in a desperate search for enemy soldiers.

There was an almighty snap just above my head as the window frame and shrank to my right in the room splintered. A series of loud snaps began to splinter our window frame and cause the contents of the shrank to burst across the room. Bobby dropped like a dead weight grabbing my smock on the way down, my face smashing into the gun as he pulled me down.

"Incoming" he screamed about the constant snapping just above us.

I looked at him as he hunkered down as small as possible; I copied him as the snapping continues to splinter the world around us. Timbers, glass, plaster, brickwork, even our beloved chairs disintegrated in front of my eyes, and the Americans were giving our position some considerable attention. The snapping was relentless, heavy gunfire from desperate men. Amid the din, Max came crawling into the room, and was getting covered in allsorts of crap from the destroyed furniture. He got close enough to be heard.

"Get that gun into the fucking fight or I will kill you myself!"

At this point, I feared the Americans more than Max, but his piercing glare soon won me over. The snapping was less frequent, so Bobby and I composed ourselves for the almost certain suicidal commitment to our window. The bipod legs of the gun were still hanging on the window ledge, I just need to lift it into my right shoulder and fight. I took a deep breath and forced myself up, swinging the gun left at the same time. The smouldering tank smoke allowed us now and again to see other burning vehicles in the street. To the right of them, I could make out muddy, olive drab shapes dashing into the buildings opposite. I fired a long burst, tracer splashing all over the front of the house, flicking skywards. Every time I saw what I felt to be enemy tank crews, I hosed the general area. Due to the smoke, I couldn't confirm the results of my marksmanship. It felt good to throw something back at them after what they just had thrown at us for the last couple of minutes. The gunfire off to our left began to subside. The thud of grenades could be heard. I didn't have a clue who was using them, but judging by the concussion, they were being used indoors. I kept my eyes on the building I'd been shooting at for a while. I couldn't see any movement. As the adrenaline began to fade, the throbbing in my nose and my top lip began to become a distraction. I'd pretty much taken a faceful of the bloody gun as Bobby pulled me down. I licked my top lip gingerly; the copper tang of blood was unmistakable. My nose felt like it was bloody huge. Keeping my eyes on the house, I pouted.

"How's my lip?"

Bobby didn't even give it a glance, "your good looks won't suffer too badly, boy."

Max scrambled into the room, kneeling down just inside the threshold,

"Good work guys, do not, I repeat, do not fire to the right of that tank in front of you, understand?"

Bobby and I nodded, as Max leaned out of the room and bellowed up the stairs for those above us to come down to the kitchen. Boot scuffs and clattering could be heard as Marco, Bruno and Karl made their way down into the kitchen. Max waved Bobby over to put him in the picture. I couldn't make out what they were saying, so I kept my eyes peeled on the house I'd been shooting up.

After a few minutes, there was activity in the kitchen; Bobby joined me back at the window at a half crawl,

"Max and the other guys are going to assault the house in front of us. Enemy tank crews are holding out in some of the buildings, so they are going to counter attack them to dislodge them from the street."

From our current position, we couldn't support them as they crossed the street, since the tank blocked our view; Bobby could read the expression on my face,

"I know Erik, just deal with the house we've been shooting up, okay?"

I remained focused on the house, totally bewildered why we couldn't reposition ourselves, maybe moving to a better vantage point could give away Max's intentions, who knows!

Before we knew it, there was a clatter of boots on cobbles as Max and his assault team sprinted across the road out of sight to us. I could hear commotion in the opposite building, the sudden thud of grenades, followed by a piercing scream. Gunfire echoed inside the target building, more grenades. I could see movement in my target building. Dark shapes bobbing around the windows on the ground floor and some of the small cellar windows beneath. Some of the dark shapes started to fire their weapons at the house Max had just assaulted. Dull muzzle flashes from way back in dark rooms. Without prompting, I fired short bursts at the offending flashes. My tracer splashed through and around the windows. Before long it wasn't just my bullets that were striking the brickwork around my targets, gunfire behind our burning tank joined in the fray. Max must be assaulting that house too.

I kept my bursts short and controlled, fearing Max and the guys would suddenly appear to the left of the tank and run straight into my fire. It wasn't long before I could just make out Max's profile appearing from behind the tank, so I switched to potential targets further to his left. Max prepared a grenade, as he went to throw it he slumped to the ground in a burst of red mist, followed straight away by the thud of his own grenade that shattered his limp frame. I hammered all the windows with everything I had. The ammunition belt on my weapon was as good as expended when I stopped firing. I looked at Max's body and then at Bobby. He kept his lips tight and put a hand on my shoulder.

"It was his time Erik," he murmured. "His war is over."

Bobby was right, of course he was, it was Max's time. Of all the people I thought would get through this awful mess, my money would have been on Max. He fought his way through Russia, France, Holland, and had managed to pass on his knowledge to us as one of our instructors on the Senne. Max was now just a shattered, bloody heap on a road in Kirchborchen. I never found out where he had come from, or if he had any family. Them snippets of information you feel can always wait for another day. It's times like this that show you how fragile life is, certainly in these situations. The popping and fizzing sparks from the tank snapped me out of it.

"Get away from the window, that thing is cooking off"

Bobby took me by the arm and pulled me back to the remains of our comfy chairs. They were in a bad way, but anything was better than sitting on the floor amongst the smashed remains of the room. I slumped into the chair, and had a grim scene to watch on top of the tank. The headless American was now getting engulfed in large licking flames. As it blackened, ammunition was cracking off inside the turret, causing it to flinch and start to slump over the heavy machine gun. What became my immediate concern was the belt of ammunition still fitted to his gun that was pointed at us. The thought of that lot going off in our direction was somewhat worrying. I nudged Bobby's arm and told him my concerns.

"Good point Erik, lets get in the kitchen."

We very quickly gathered up our weapons and equipment and scurried into the kitchen. Our other panzer crewmen were gathered in the kitchen making coffee. Our squad was now rather depleted; it was basically now just me and this panzer crew. Bobby made both of us a coffee, and then address his crew.

"How we doing for ammo?" It wasn't directed at anyone in particular.

"Couple of magazines per man", one of his boys piped up, "couple of grenades between us, no more Panzerfaust."

Bobby grabbed hold of the very short belt of ammo left on the machine gun.

"Is this the last of it?"

I nodded.

"This isn't going to get us very far," he looked at his crew," let's see if there is anything of use upstairs."

All of us made our way upstairs. Two fairly large rooms overlooked the street. The right hand room was clearly meant for children, toys, trinkets on the various wooden units. Two small beds at either end of the room. The room was coated in dust with numerous bullet strikes in the high side of the right wall. The wooden shutters we badly smashed and hanging from the fittings. Large chunks of brickwork and masonry we missing from the street side wall, and we scattered all over the room. Glass was evident all over the place aswell. Who ever had to fight from this room received some serious incoming from the Americans. Outside the window, a heavy light grey smoke drifted up from the tank; cause the building behind to shimmer. The odd flame would flick up to our window, as the headless American was now just a funeral pyre, the heavy scent of cooked meat hung heavily in the air. I didn't want to look at it, so I kept back from the window besides, some trigger happy American waiting to take a shot.

Movement caught my eye in the house beyond the smoke. I crouched fearing it being American, but I quickly recognised the profile of Bruno. He was looking straight at me waving frantically. I gave him a thumbs up, which he returned, all appeared well over there. I called out onto the landing.

"Bobby, we've got friendlies in the house opposite."

He peered around the doorway. "How many?"

"I don't know", I replied "I don't want to shout to them and draw attention."

Bobby nodded, we didn't know what the Americans had in store for us, and besides, we needed them back over this side of the road. Bobby put his hand on my shoulder,

"Follow me; we need them back over here."

I followed him downstairs and out the back of the house. We skirted around the right side, stopping short of the corner, the front of the Sherman just about level with us. Bobby gestured for me to stay put, he then continued forward at a crouch in front of the Sherman. He then stopped and peered around the tank. I watched him wave and give them over the road a thumbs up. He than frantically waved them over. I could hear the rapid clatter of boots on cobbles as Bruno and Karl came scampering around past Bobby. Just as they got past Bobby, red tracer snapped and whizzed off the cobbles just in front of him, causing them to flick up and smash into the house to our right.

Bobby jumped back, lost his footing and landed on his arse. He quickly turned and scrambled back to the three of us. He let out a nervous giggle.

"That was fucking close", he took hold of the other lads by their smocks," you guys okay?"

They both nodded, "Marco is dead, they took his head off as we got in through the ground floor window, Max dealt with them fuckers."

Max, our leader, now just another dead soldier in the middle of the street.

Bobby led us back to the kitchen, and got us back upstairs. The only ammunition we had was whatever was left around the house and on our bodies. It was late morning, and with any luck we would get fresh troops and ammo pretty soon. Down the street to our left towards the bridge, the odd thud of a grenade or a burst of gunfire broke up the silence every now and again. The only constant in our lives right now, was the cracking and popping of the Sherman below our window. Taking caution, I would try and peer left, and see if there were any movement in the other houses opposite. I couldn't help but look at Max. Still lying there, in full view. Such a shame. There were dead Americans in the street aswell, but it didn't really register in my head. They appeared as muddy green piles of rags will helmets, but Max look like a bloodied, drunken soldier asleep where he fell.

The day continued throughout with not so much movement or action. It was the end of March, and therefore wasn't particularly warm. I decided to use the children's bed clothes to drape over my shoulders to take the cold edge off. Before long, the light outside started to fade. Bobby moved about the house, doing his rounds, seeing we were all ok. I found it rather bizarre, a few hours ago, he was bailing out of his panzer, and quickly drafted into the infantry, and was now our squad leader. I suppose that's war for you.

Bobby peered into the room, "I'm going to try and find out what we are going to be doing tonight, don't waste anymore ammo or grenades unless you can hit what you are shooting at, okay?"

"Sure", I nodded, "could you try and scrounge some ammo for this."

I gave the MG42 a light kick for him to get the idea.

"I will try; I will be back as soon as I can." With that, he made his way downstairs. I didn't want to sit on my own any longer, so I gathered up the gun, and my equipment, and joined Bruno and Karl in the adjoining room. I found them sitting on the master bed. Bruno perched on the end keeping watch out of the window, and Karl sat up against the head of the bed, with the bed clothes wrapped around him dozing. I sat next to Bruno on the end.

"Are you guys okay? Pretty intense eh?"

Bruno gave me a tight lipped smile, his eyes glazed, probably both through emotion and exhaustion.

"Hopefully we will get some more guys and ammunition shortly, I don't think we have the muscle right now to fend off the Americans again."

I agreed with him. SS or not, ammo and manpower was always a factor, since without either, we were going to get overrun sooner or later. I didn't have much to talk about, and I didn't want to talk about how Marco got killed. What did play on my mind was what Bobby had told me last night. Our exploits in the name of the Fuhrer and the Fatherland. I chose not to repeat it, since I was unsure of Bruno's loyalties or political awareness. Such gossip around the wrong people could have you in a whole heap of trouble, so I kept it to myself. I settled for no small talk and just paid attention to what was going on out in the street, and to sum it up very quickly, nothing.

It was almost dark when I heard movement downstairs, followed by a familiar voice.

"Guys, grab all your gear and get down here." It was Bobby.

Bruno gave Karl a shove, who slowly emerged from the bedclothes and gathered up his fighting gear. We trudged downstairs and met Bobby and his panzer crew in the kitchen. The crewmen passed around a few cups of coffee. Bobby called for quiet.

"Gentlemen, we are withdrawing back into Paderborn."

He paused to allow his opening statement to sink in.

"We will establish a new defence line between Kirchborchen and Paderborn. I've just been talking to the Hauptsturmfuhrer a few houses down, and he has made the decision for us to move there, due to lack of manpower and ammunition. He is confident we have slowed the Americans down to a more cautious pace, and now is the right time to break from this engagement."

We just looked at each other, some of us nodding. We gathered up our gear and weapons and followed Bobby out into the back garden. It wasn't very big, with almost a sheer high rock ledge marking the end of the garden. Off to our right, in the half light, I could see friendly troops slowly making their way along the base of the rock ledge, some carrying the wounded, and the remainder appeared to be in reasonable shape. At the head of the column was a rather well built SS officer, the Hauptsturmfuhrer Bobby had spoken of. He turned and gestured for the column to stop and rest. The group was a mixed bag of SS infantry, black clad panzer crewmen, minus the panzers, and a few random troops thrown in aswell. The officer approached our small group; I decided to keep my mouth shut whilst he spoke to Bobby.

"Oberscharfuhrer, I'm not in the business of wasting lives in a fruitless attempt at keeping the wolf from the door, I hope you understand." He stated quietly.

Bobby nodded, "I understand, Hauptsturmfuhrer."

The officer continued, "We will leave here quietly and make our way towards the north end of town. We will link up with reserves and armour. We can then get our wounded seen to, and the remainder of us fed and watered, and with abit of luck, more ammunition."

"Yes, Hauptsturmfuhrer." Bobby nodded. The officer continued,

"I will take the lead, could you please bring up the rear, I don't want any of our wounded being left for the Americans, thank you."

The officer turned to his battered column, waving them forward. They slowly clambered to their feet, the wounded groaning, their helpers hushing them. The officer moved off slowly, his column of tired, broken men shuffling behind him. We chose to remain with Bobby at the rear since we had all gotten used to each others company. Hopefully, we would be well clear of here when the Americans realised we had withdrawn north towards Paderborn. No doubt we would have the pleasure of their company again soon enough. But for now, I was confident we had smashed them to a standstill.

Progress was painfully slow as we climbed our way out of Kirchborchen. Many times on the march, the column would stop, soldiers would take turns carrying the wounded on makeshift stretchers of old household doors, or whatever was strong and rigid enough to do the job. The wounded were amazing; some of them looked in a real bad way. I don't think there was a single medic in the column, so there was no pain relief to be had, and they stifled their own groans and moans. If I was wounded, I would bite my lip tight, no matter how much pain I was in. I would not want to be left for the Americans. I can't imagine they would give a wounded SS soldier anything, apart from a bullet to the head.

As we made our way out of town, we would now and again stop and just listen to anything that could potentially be following us, by that I mean American infantry. The wounded kept quite whilst we just tuned into the environment. Every so often, there would be a dull pop of ammunition cooking off in the knocked out vehicles down on the road. Satisfied that there was no one following us, we would gather our flock and continue trudging out of town. We would continue to stop and start, but for various reasons. Stretcher bearers would change over, and we now began to encounter other small groups of friendly forces. They had nothing but what they stood up in, and whatever ammunition and weapons they could carry. At least we had the relative luxury of some armour, be it just for a short time. It was a good job we didn't encounter some itchy trigger fingers in these groups, since it was very dark now and it could all go wrong very quickly. The officer would have a chat with whoever was in command of the groups and we would then move on.

The column came to a standstill once again; the guys carrying the wounded were starting to run out of steam. Bobby gave our small group a nod and a wink to take our turn. The previous stretcher bearers took our weapons so we just had to deal with the soldier strapped to the door. I took up the rear right position. Once we were all set to go, we lifted our man, and trudged on. The route up and out of town was bloody hard work. The officer was leading us through a maze of houses and gardens, which appeared to do nothing more than just make the whole ordeal longer. I felt exposed with out my weapon. All I had to defend myself at this present time was two stick grenades stuffed into my belt. I was starting to really sweat now, I could feel it trickling down my temples and run along the inside of my chinstrap. Progress was slow, but we got ourselves into a marching rhythm. We would change over quickly, even when the officer hadn't stopped the column for a rest.

As we made our way up into the top end of town, the ground started to level out. What wasn't helping us in our march was the fact that we were now entering the outer limits of Paderborn. The city had its fair share of bomb damage. Kirchborchen had pretty much got away unscathed, unlike Paderborn, which was smashed like you wouldn't believe. We had to take care we wouldn't slip on the loose surface of bricks, timber, and exposed pipe work from sewers etc. The familiar scent of human shit was now present, since the sewer pipes were also shattered. Bruno lost his footing and crumpled to the ground. Our wounded comrade gasped, but to his credit, made no more of a fuss. Bruno apologised and got himself together. Once ready, we continued. Progress was painfully slow, both in the biblical sense, and in our hands and shoulders.

We found our way onto the main road out of Kirchborchen, which was just about recognisable, due to all the shattered remains of buildings strewn all over it. Up ahead, I noticed some black and dusty panzer crewman clambering all over a large pile of bricks and masonry. As we drew closer, it became clear that this pile of bricks had a tank barrel sticking out of it. One of the crewmen stood on the backside of it caught my gaze and gave me the same casual salute I received before. We were now back with the Jadgpanther that helped us out yesterday morning. Its crew had taken the time to camouflage it with the ruins that surrounded it. We trudged past the Jadgpanther and continued on further about another 300 metres. The officer called for us to stop and take a breather. We carefully placed our wounded man down on the ground, and then I found myself somewhere to take the weight off my feet and have a drink. The remaining water in my bottle was just enough to take the edge off my thirst; hopefully I would get a chance soon to refill it soon. I peeled my helmet off; a cool breeze swept over may head instantly. My hair was quite long on top but I kept the sides cropped short. It was all matted with sweat from the effort of our march, but after running my fingers through it a few times, it felt somewhat more comfortable.

The officer came walking down the line, stating that we were to get the wounded over to a halftrack just a little further up the road. We gathered ourselves up quickly, and with our wounded cargo, we carefully followed the officer to the halftrack in question. Once loaded onboard, we ensured the wounded were stripped of any weapons and ammunition that would be of more use to us than them. The halftrack gunned its engine, and its crew slowly pulled away, crunching over the smashed debris from houses scattered in its path. The officer then led us back down to near where we had taken a rest. We then branched off to the left and took up our fighting positions amongst the rubble. Where we were sited, our field of view was once again, not that great. Directly in front of us at about 200 meters, was the Jagdpanther, its back decks and exhaust recognisable in the low light. Only its front and sides were coated in the remains of someone's home.

Our group of battered and bruised men were all strung out in a line of sorts, with the officer and Bobby positioned rear centre. They were deep in conversation, various nods and shaking of heads were all that gave it away. Bobby then got to his feet and moved over to the right end of the line, gathering one of his former panzer crew in the process. With that, they walked away down the road toward Paderborn, out of sight. On the horizon, dawn was not far away. I took this as my opportunity to try and get comfortable and rest, I was completely shattered, but sleep would not come easily, too many things going through my head. As I slowly began to relax, the cold started to creep in. We no longer had the luxury of a roof over our heads, but it was a clear night, which brought in the chilled air.

Every now and again, I would drift off, waking with a violent shiver. I had only the clothing I was currently wearing, and I regretted not bringing the child's bedclothes with me. We had pretty much passed the point of looking mean and fearsome; I just wanted to keep warm. I propped my self up on one elbow, and could make out some of the guys had a cigarette on the go. I wasn't a smoker, but I had to admit, it did give you an illusion of warmth. Away in the far distance, I could make out the sound of tank fire and the chatter of machine guns. I wasn't overly concerned, since it was some distance away. Some other poor soul was clearly fighting for his life trying to keep the Americans at bay. All was quite here. For now.

Slowly but surely, the light around us began to give away what It had hidden in the darkness. I adjusted my seating position so I was now looking forward towards the back end of the Jagdpanther. Off to the right of it across the road was one of our flak guns. The darkness slowly revealed the subtle profile of the guys that manned it. The odd glow of a cigarette confirming what I was looking at. Movement to my right caught my attention. Level with us, but on the other side of the road, appeared to be another squad of infantry. About ten of them altogether, and judging by their appearance and equipment, could well have been SS. Most were wounded in one way or another. Bandages featured with most of them, blood could clearly be seen soaking through some of them.

I scanned up and down our line. There was no sign of Bobby, who had been gone some time now. I didn't know what type of errand the officer had sent him on, hopefully to find us some ammunition. Up ahead, I noticed movement on the engine decks of the Jagdpanther. One of its crew was hunched over the top of the vehicle, as he turned to address his crew who were asleep behind the vehicle, I could make out he was holding binoculars.

"Tanks and Infantry leaving the quarry!" He hollered back at us. Here we go again.

The officer came scrambling down our line at a half crouch, giving those who were dozing a rough shove. Like automatons, our group checked their weapons, and were putting their grenades on the front of their parapet, ready for action. The MG42 in my possession had literally just about ten rounds of belt left attached to it, and my two grenades completed my means of fighting. This was not good, unless Bobby came back real soon with some ammunition; we were going to be in for some real trouble soon. There was a crunching of masonry and loud cursing behind us, and over the rubble mound to our rear came Bobby and his crewman, dragging a large, flat wooden crate between them. They slumped in a sweaty heap behind me, exhausted.

"Erik", Bobby managed between gasps of breath, "find me a cigarette!"

Without hesitation, I scrambled up the line towards were the remainder of his panzer crew were set up. They anticipated my arrival, before I got to ask them, they produced a rather dog eared cigarette, and a badly creased book of matches. I thanked them, and made my way back towards my previous position. As I drew close to Bobby and the wooden crate, the officer was stood over him, with a grenade in each hand. He threw them roughly back into the crate.

"Are they fucking serious!" he hissed, "we've got tanks and infantry approaching us, and them fat, lazy bastards back there give us just a box of fucking potato mashers!" Potato mashers referred to the shape of our grenades. The explosive core at one end, mounted on a thick wooden stem.

"Apologies Hauptsturmfuhrer", Bobby murmured, crestfallen. "That's all they would give us."

The officer knelt down next to him. "It's not your fault, Oberscharfuhrer. It just angers me when the idiots sipping cognac back there expect us to hold the Americans at bay with just a box of grenades."

I took it as my cue to approach them with Bobby's cigarette. Bobby looked up and grinned.

"Thank you Erik, could you dish out these to all the lads in our line", he gave the crate a kick.

"Sure." I didn't try and drag the heavy crate over the rubble, so I just grabbed a cluster of them with both hands, and started at one end of the line and worked my way down. I was a sweaty, smelly mess when they were all finally distributed. Everyone had three or four each. Not much to stop tanks, but that's all we had.

## 8.

I settled back into my fighting position, just awaiting the inevitable. It wasn't too far away, the streaking roar of panzerfausts back down in Kirchborchen announced the arrival of more Americans. The muffled thud of rockets meeting their targets was instantly followed up by the chattering of MG42, no one could mistake that sound. The soundtrack down in the town suddenly changed to the overwhelming thunder of tank fire. The Americans had raised their game by the sound of things. We sat amongst the rubble, listening to the streak of our rockets, followed instantly by the roar of tank fire. The Americans must have been pulverising our friendly forces that we passed through last night. The tank fire would cease for a short while, and the silence would be filled by the muffled thud of grenades. American Infantry in the houses. Rifle fire, screaming, shouting. More tank fire would drown out the plight of the Infantry. It all sounded rather horrendous. Then tank fire continued on for quite some time. I could only guess how on earth our friendly forces could extract themselves out of that carnage, if at all.

The fighting down in Kirchborchen would succumb to silence. All I could hear were troops shouting in a language I could not understand. The Americans were clearly not getting run out of town by us today. Engine noise became the theme of Kirchborchen. More streaking of rockets, even more tank fire. Up ahead of us, the Jagdpanther crew scrambled into their vehicle. Here we go. Over to the right, the flak gun crew were now up and moving, getting ready for action. My stomach tightened and turned over. In my short military career, I could safely say I'd just had my fair share of combat, but I doubt you ever fight off the pre-match nerves. I slipped my helmet back on. I looked either side of me; everyone else was ready to go. The officer was scampering up and down the line, giving us all a friendly pat on the shoulder and thumbs up. The loud thud of the Jagdpanther's gun announced its entry into the fight. It rocked back on its suspension, bricks and masonry fell off its sides. It fired once again, more of its camouflage crumbled away. Almost instantly, it violently rocked back in a flurry of sparks and shattered brick work. The Americans had it in their sights. In quick succession, it was struck numerous times by unseen forces, sparks flying off the front of its thick armour. The house debris it was covered in was splintered and shattered all over the front of its position, and the flak gun crew. The Jagdpanther continued to rock back on its suspension, taking all that the Americans could throw at it. Black smoke began to creep out of its engine decks. Its dusty, black clad crewmen scrambled out of the top of it. They rolled off the back of the smouldering vehicle and scampered over to our line, jumping into my position. They were sweating and breathing heavily. The officer crawled over to check they were okay. What appeared to be the commander of the panzer nodded.

"Yes Hauptsturmfuhrer, it would have been a damn sight better if we had some fucking ammunition and fuel. We couldn't move it, hence the camouflage."

They were all armed with MP40, their sub machine guns, and wasted no time in joining us in our line, scrambling furiously to build up their fighting positions with whatever was available around them, bricks, splintered timber, anything that gave them half a chance of some sort of protection. The smoke pouring out of the Jadgpanther was now getting thicker and blacker. Flames began to lick out of the engine decks. The Jadg crew could do nothing more than just watch her succumb to the flames that began to overwhelm her. Judging by what the commander had just said, there was no ammunition or fuel left to cook off, so it would just be its fittings going up in flames.

The flak gun burst into life with a rapid, thumping drum beat, as its crew members fed it with large clips of ammunition. Without prompting, the squad of Infantry opposite sprung into life and dashed across in front of us and began to crawl around behind the burning tank destroyer. One of them peered over the rubble to his front, beckoning his men to line up alongside him. They all then, as one man, threw grenades over the rubble pile. A series of loud thuds then echoed, and they all stood up, firing their weapons and charged over the mound, out of sight. In between the heavy rapid fire of the flak gun, I could make out the report of rifle and sub machine gun fire. Familiar sounds from our range days on the Senne. The squad clearly took it upon themselves to counter attack, remarkable, but potentially suicidal.

 The flak gun burst back into life. The crew was really going for it, against who we couldn't see. Amongst the rubble around the burning tank someone was throwing small objects back at them. It became horrifyingly clear what was happening when those objects exploded around the flak crew, obscuring them in a dust cloud of brick and masonry. As the dust drifted off, the flak gun stood silent, its crew nowhere to be seen.

"Infantry!" screamed some of the guys to the right of the line.

I turned to focus on the burning tank, I couldn't see anything, but those that had called out were already firing in that direction. Their rounds splashing all over the stricken vehicle and the rubble around it, which caused the dust to flick up, and their tracer to scream off in all directions. I still couldn't see anything.

"Slightly left of the tank!" someone roared.

I adjusted my gaze, and sure as shit, I could see what could have been the mud smeared domes of American helmets. Everyone less me started firing, their rounds splashing all around the offending shapes. I started throwing my grenades in their direction. As they exploded just short of my target, I prayed that the splinters they gave off found their targets. I couldn't really tell. More of these mud smeared, olive drab domes began to bob around in the rubble around the tank.

"Prepare to withdraw!" roared the officer, "when I say so, throw all of your grenades and follow me!"

I had thrown mine and I now just hunched down in my fighting position. I could see the other guys preparing to throw theirs. Bullets snapped over our heads, smashing into the broken brickwork behind us. Rounds screamed off in all directions as they clipped the masonry. The snapping over our heads began to become really intense, I had my head tucked well behind cover. Above me stood the officer, his rifle in the shoulder, firing away at our enemy. Rounds were smashing all over our position, yet there he stood, in full view of the Americans, pouring it back at them. I felt it was only a matter of time before their aim got good, and his luck got bad. The audible clunk of his magazine becoming empty didn't even faze him; he merely looked left and right.

"NOW!" he roared.

Everyone in the line got on one knee and lobbed their grenades as far and as fast as they could. I knelt up and looked towards where I had seen the enemy in the rubble. Our grenades burst all around them, dust and brick splinters coating them. The officer was on his feet sprinting up and over the rubble to our rear, our guys sprinting off after him. I didn't need any prompting for this next move; I scrambled out of my hole and pushed as hard as I could through the loose house debris. The snapping of rounds was very loud in my ears as the Americans tried to cut us down in our mad dash out of there. I crested the rubble pile and could see the lads strung out, with the officer leading back towards were we had put the wounded on the halftrack earlier that morning. A halftrack appeared from behind one of the shattered houses to the right. The officer waved it down, and I don't know what he said to its crew, they were quickly un-coupling another halftrack that appeared to have broken down. My lungs were burning as I pressed on to the vehicle. I didn't want to look back, fearing American troops had made it to the crest of the mound and it was now just a case of picking us off as we sprinted for the halftrack. My ankles turned in the rubble, which made me wince, but I couldn't afford to slow down. I reached the rear of the halftrack, as the officer was helping get the guys up and into the back. When it came to my turn, he gripped me by my smock.

"Where the fuck is the machine gun, soldier?"

I was stunned, totally stunned. I had abandoned my weapon to the enemy, the look of rage on his face gave away the fact I had really fucked up. I didn't know what to say, I couldn't think straight. What possessed me to leave the MG42 behind?

He released my smock, and took off in the direction we had just come. Bobby was stood up in the back of the halftrack.

"What the hell is he doing?" I just couldn't find the words to explain my crime.

The officer scrambled up and over the rubble out of sight. As soon as he crested the rubble, the sheer volume of gun fire on the other side was almost overwhelming. Had the officer just gone to his death? The sheer weight of fire as he crested the mound would have suggested so. We couldn't see what was happening, but it was as if the entire world was ending just the other side of the rubble mound. What have you got yourself into here Erik?

A lone figure appeared on the crest and came scrambling down towards us. The profile of the officer became more recognisable, and in his hands he had the MG42. As he jogged up to the halftrack, he stuffed it broadside into my crest, winding me in the process.

"Don't ever do that again, do you understand soldier?" He glared at me.

"Yes Hauptsturmfuhrer." It was all I could muster, I couldn't believe he survived going back to retrieve it.

He looked up at the rest of the guys. "Let's get the fuck out of here." With that he walked around to the front cab and I quickly heaved myself into the vehicle. I doubt he felt the same way about leaving me behind. The halftrack lurched forward and we got the hell out of there.

The halftrack lurched, creaked, and rattled through the shattered streets on the outskirts of Paderborn. The bombing two nights previous had really taken it out of the city. As we slowly grinded through the shattered maze of streets, I was amazed how the local residents were working hard, without any real direction, clearing the roads of rubble and other debris from the raid. We could clearly identify the road in which we travelled on. Off to the flanks, there were neat piles of bricks and other materials that had remained intact and maybe could be reused in an eventual rebuild. Military traffic was light and orderly. Military Police were manning the main intersections, directing troops and vehicles alike through the destruction. The civilians paid no attention to us; they had more pressing issues, such as recovering what they held dear from their smashed houses. I couldn't see any dead bodies at the roadside. Maybe that terrible chore had already been dealt with the day before, whilst we dealt with the Americans in Kirchborchen.

I caught the gaze of Bobby, who did nothing more than give me a nod and a wink. He looked tired; in fact we were all pretty tired. It had been a while since we had anything real decent to eat; my last proper meal was in Senne before the march to Kirchborchen. Some of the other guys packed in with us were dozing, but you can't beat a good night's sleep in a real bed. When we would see a bed again was anyone's guess, the Americans were too close for us to rest our heads on a pillow. It was merely a case of just closing your eyes and just bumping and rolling with the motion of the Halftrack.

Not too sure how long I was dozing, but a rough shove brought me round with a start. As I focused on the guys around me, I noticed the officer leaning over towards us, the remainder of the guys looking at him.

'We are trading space for time', he shouted over the rattling din of engine and tank tracks. 'We are moving north to Schlangen, just the other side of Bad Lip. We plan to meet up with fragmented units plus Panzers from the north. Paderborn is now untenable to us with such few numbers, so we are putting in a defence line at Schlangen so we can contain the Americans in Paderborn, understand?'

We just nodded at him; in return he just eyed us suspiciously, probably not entirely convinced that we understood what he just told us. From what I could take into my exhausted brain, we were going to hold the line up at Schlangen, and wait for reinforcements. I liked them type of plans, simple and easy to remember. I just wanted us to be far enough away from Bad Lip when the shooting started, since Mother was still there in our home. Bad Lip held nothing of value to the Americans as far as I was concerned, Paderborn being the prize I'm sure.

As we headed north towards Marienloh, the going got better since the bombers had dropped their ordinance on Paderborn. The only reason our pace was slow was due to the sheer volume of people traffic on the road. Soldiers marching in groups of various sizes. Women, children, and the elderly with all that they could carry and cram into baby carriages. This concerned me somewhat, since they were moving up to where we could potentially encounter the

Americans next. I just hoped they would just keep walking until they were well passed our next positions.

We made slow progress through the river of civilians. Troops on the streets were gesturing them to get out of the way and let military traffic pass. It didn't have much of an effect, they just carried on walking. Slowly and painfully, we began to make progress, the crowd thinning out, and we could speed up some what. It wasn't long before we were entering Bad Lip, my home town. I was suddenly overwhelmed by home sickness. There I was, dirty and tired, sat in the back of a halftrack, trundling through my neighbourhood, with my home and mother merely a few streets over, truly bizarre. Our vehicle lurched to a halt. People traffic once again causing the hold up. Very quickly, I had a revelation. I could just jump out of this bloody machine, and sprint my heart out down the alleyways, and vanish. The guys sat with me wouldn't know what was happening until it was over. I could do it, no problem.

But the fearful dread of reprisal then overwhelmed me. What if I was followed or the Military Police received information regarding where I lived. Punishment would be swift and ruthless. Mother may be punished, for hiding a deserter. They would not take pity on her for hiding her boy from the war. I couldn't risk mother being dragged into my error of judgement. I chose to stay put in the halftrack. We then lurched forward again, and crept our way through the people flooded streets. We very slowly cleared Bad Lip which despite my feeling of self pity was a good move. I'm glad our masters did not want to make a stand there. We pushed north, our speed dictated by the civilians fleeing the fighting.

## 9.

The people traffic slowly began to lighten. We were just south of the village of Schlangen, when the sound of a small aircraft caught my attention. It was overcast, but the cloud base was quite high, and I could clearly see a small single prop aircraft buzzing around off to our right. It was the first aircraft I had seen for some time, it was too far away however to tell who it belonged to. It drifted closer to our line of march on the road, and it was clearly not a bomber or fighter. I gave it no more of my time and went back to taking interest in the state of my unpolished, badly scuffed boots. I would be reprimanded for such turnout if we were still in Senne under instruction. Our instructors, in which one of them would have been Max, would have come down on us harshly for such cases of poor discipline. Given the circumstances, I don't think anyone around here was going to lose much sleep over the state of my boots right now.

We rattled and squealed our way through Schlangen until we were out of the northern end. Apart from a few isolated buildings and fenced fields were back out into open farmland. We past an intersection and it was then I noticed more friendly troops milling about, and a couple of panzers were sited facing back into Schlangen with the front of them tucked into the raised bank of the road that ran off toward the Teutoburg Wald and Berlebeck, a small village, sat on the backside of the hills the Teutoburg ran along. The halftrack lurched off to the left side of the road and bumped uncomfortably out Into the field behind the panzers and turned left so we ended up facing Schlangen once again. The officer stood up, let off an almighty stretch, scratched his arse, and clambered off the vehicle. He appeared once more at the rear.

'Sit tight, whilst I find us a spot to get set up. We should expect reinforcements from the north anytime soon. The Americans will take their time picking their way through Paderborn. By the time they realise there is no one to fight, our reinforcements should be here, and we can go back into town and give them what for.'

With that, he set off. The guys in with me began to come to life, slowly dragging their tired frames from the halftrack, stretching their legs, allowing the circulation in their numb arses and legs get flowing again. It wasn't long before we heard a wolf whistle, and we turned to see the officer waving at us and beckoning us over to him. The position he had for us was about 100 metres off to the right of the two panzers wedged into the bank, their crews applying turf to the front and sides, leaving their turrets poking over the top of the high banked road. He called the halftrack crew forward with their vehicle aswell, siting the vehicle how he wanted it before siting us in pairs along the bank. I was paired up with Bobby once again.

The Hauptsturmfuhrer put us to task, letting us know how he wanted us to maintain our position. Our center of mass would be the halftrack, which had an MG42, plus some ammunition mounted in its small turret. Its appointed gunner would man this position, and its driver would become another infantryman dug into the bank with us. We were to camouflage the vehicle as best we could with local materials, but leave the turret free to traverse, should it need to engage targets on the flanks. Once the halftrack was dealt with, we were to dig our selves in to the bank.
Once we had finished our battle positions, I was just a sweat soaked mess. I didn't smell too great. My belt kit had that pungent aroma of soaked leather that would stiffen as it dried, which made it a real pain to get back on. I took my helmet off and rested against the bank. I ran my fingers through my sweaty matt of hair, and once again noticed the little aircraft buzzing around. It was quite a welcome site, since all I'd seen up to this point was chaos, death and sorrow. It gave me a sense of carefree abandon, to just glide

about at your leisure without a care in the world. Not too sure what purpose the little aircraft had in this area, but nor did I really care.

For some time, there was a steady stream of civilians passing through our position. Were they fleeing the fighting, or the supposed raping, murdering American hordes following them? The little information I knew about the Americans as a whole said nothing about their brutal methods. I knew of Hollywood and their movie stars. There was a quietly murmured admiration for their logistics and firepower that some of our instructors had witnessed first hand in Normandy and during our withdrawal from France. Willi had written to mother, and in none of his letters was there any real reason to fear them, unless you happen to be fighting them. They hated the SS, that was no secret, and by the stories Bobby told me recently, they were not the only ones with a hatred for us. From what I could gather, there was no love lost between us and the Army guys either and we were meant to be on the same side. I didn't want to sound defeatist, but I wasn't confident about the possibility of sanctuary when this whole horrible war finally played out. I was dug in on a raised bank, not far from my own home, with the enemy not too far away. What have you got yourself into here Erik?

I felt a shove, which made me jump. Bobby was knelt over me grinning.

'You snore like a fucking freight train, boy.'

I made my apologies, and sat myself up leaning against the bank. I fumbled for my water battle. There wasn't much left, so I gulped down the remainder. It felt good, despite the chill in the air. I was hungry, but to be fair, find me someone around here that wasn't. The flow of civilian traffic that trudged through our position had now reduced to lone individuals and the occasional pair of sorry looking old folk now and then. Over to my right I could see the officer talking to one of the panzer crews. Judging by his body language, he appeared rather agitated. The panzer crewman up on his vehicle would shake his head, with the occasional shrug of his shoulders. The officer then spun on his heels and began trudging up towards us. He called for Bobby with a wave, in which Bobby responded to immediately. With the quick exchange of nodding heads, and muted dialogue from the officer, Bobby then went to each of our positions to rouse the men.

Word come down the line for us all to converge on the officer who had knelt down next to his own fighting position. As I found a spot to kneel down, he had his map unfolded on the ground between us. A small, crudely sharpened pencil in his hand.

'The Americans have halted in Marienloh. Not too sure why, probably supply issues, and the ambush threat.'

He paused, glanced at us, and then continued.

'We are here, just on the northern edge of Schlangen. Behind us is Kohlstadt. We are due to receive reinforcements. They will be moving south through Kohlstadt anytime soon. We have been told to expect Tigers, 88's, and Infantry, so if you notice movement behind us, make sure you can tell who they are before you decide to open fire, understand?'

We nodded. I was rather relieved we would be getting more troops and Tigers shortly. Just as we were getting to our feet, Bobby raised a hand and called for order. Silence fell upon us instantly.

'Hauptsturmfuhrer, what shape are the panzers in we have right now?'

The officer shook his head.

'They've no fuel, and only a few rounds between them. Machine gun ammo they have plenty of, but not much to kill armour with.'

Bobby nodded, tight lipped. Not ideal at all.

What became apparent was that the little, annoying aircraft was still loitering off to the east. It can be safely said, that this little aircraft had been buzzing around us throughout our move north out of Paderborn, and continued to do so. I noticed Bobby look up at the aircraft, and then look around him in, his face drain of all colour.

'Get in your holes' Bobby barked.

We looked at him, and each other. The officers' face dropped from a confident glare to one of horror.

Back towards Paderborn, there was a low rumble of thunder. Followed instantly by an ever increasing screech. There was a very loud thud to the rear of our position. I turned as blast rippled through our position, winding us all, punching the dust off our uniforms. I saw a huge fountain of grey, along with huge chunks of earth. There was a second screech, this time the shell hit the road, showering gravel, and mud high into the air, half the distance from the last strike. As the blast rippled through us, it felt as if Id just been kicked in the testicles. The burning in my stomach was intense.

'Get in your fucking holes, get away from the tanks!' roared Bobby.

I didn't need any more encouragement. I got to my feet, but the cramp in my stomach would only allow me to run at a crouch. As I got to my fighting position, blast swept through again, punching me in the back, my ears ringing. I tumbled head first into my hole. As I got myself sorted out, I turned to see the last shower of earth raining down between the static panzers.

They've found their mark, here it comes.

Because of the ringing in my ears, I felt it before I heard it. I hunkered down in my hole as tight as I could. The ground beneath me thudded with such a force, I bounced, and it was really giving my back a pummelling. Over the top of me, blast rippled through our position, every time it felt as if I was being punched in the stomach, and the testicles. My world was just a dust storm of punches to my entire body, as if God himself was punishing me. As the ringing in my ears began to fade another shell strike would make them ring again. The biblical thuds into the ground continued, but not right on top of us as they had first started out. Someone else on our position was subject to the wrath of American firepower.

As the dust around my position began to settle, and my hearing returned, I got up onto my knees, and peered out of the hole. One of the panzers was smouldering badly. I could make out broken heaps of soldiers that, by the looks of things, were caught in the open. I couldn't tell who was alive in my immediate area, was I alone? I slowly got to my feet, dirt and dust falling from me as I moved. My exposed skin was rough to the touch, glazed in dirt from it sticking to my sweat. I moved over to the nearest panzer, its local camouflage was blown clear exposing the profile of the vehicle. To the right of me, were the remnants of the other guys fighting positions. The raised road had partially collapsed, burying those who, like me sought refuge in their holes. There was no evidence of my squad, until suddenly the loose earth covering one position started to fall away. The profile of an arm became clear, then a shoulder, the rim of a helmet, an ear, nose, it was Bobby, rising from the grave, and I was transfixed, watching this amazing demonstration of survival before me.

Bobby fought his way halfway out of his grave, then noticed me stood there.

'Are you going to just stand there, or give me a fucking hand boy?'

At first his words didn't register in my brain, he then outstretched his hand.

'Fucking help then!'

I snapped out my trance, dashing forward to help him. He'd managed to get his torso out from the crushing weight of soil and gravel, but I had to help him claw away at the sucking soil trap that had his legs entombed. In a few minutes he was out of his supposed grave, both of us laying flat on our backs, gasping for breath. We didn't speak for a couple of minutes, what could I say to a man than was buried alive but a few minutes ago? Bobby had taken everything the Fuhrer had thrown at him, and more, so it was only fair to give the man a couple of minutes to compose himself. Out of the corner of my eye I could see him rooting through his pockets, producing a very sorry looking cigarette, placing it between his lips.

'Erik, do you have a light?'

'No, besides, those things are bad for you.'

We began to giggle, Bobbys' quickly turning into a hacking cough. He got himself up onto his knees; hand flat on his thighs, taking in the scene around him. I sat myself up, began to beat the dirt and dust from my smock. It fell from every crease in my uniform. Bobby looked no better. We both stood up, taking turns to beat the loose soil from our uniforms and equipment. Once we'd done as much as we felt possible, I heard the squeaky creek of metal. I spun around and noticed the top hatch of the panzer nearest us. A set of hands appeared above the hatch periscopes, and then a head appeared, followed by the black sweaty dusty frame of one of its crew men. He scrambled out over onto the back engine decks, hiding behind his turret. Bobby let out a short, sharp whistle, which caught his attention.

'Guys, the Americans are literally straight down that road' he spoke quietly,' I can see armour, but no infantry. I've got nothing to fire at them, bastards!'

Max and I began to make our way over to the back of the panzer, the vehicle instantly lurched back on its running gear, with an almighty thud, huge sparks showering us. A piercing ring screamed through my head, I dropped to my knees, cupping my ears. I noticed the crewman on the back decks was rolling around in the grass behind the vehicle smouldering, one of his legs a ragged mess, face all bloody. The panzer lurched with another muffled thud, more sparks showered the area. I lay on my belly, I saw Bobby dash over to the burning crewman, who grabbed Bobby's dusty black tunic, a pleading look on his face. Bobby nodded frantically; gripping the burning mans wrists and pulling his hands free.

My hearing returned, the crackling of a burning vehicle was the first thing I registered. Bobby scrambled over to me, barking orders at me.

'Grenade, give it to me.'

I looked down at my belt kit, I had grenades tucked into it, but in my punch drunk state, I was stuck as to which one to give him. Bobby's patience was short, grabbing the closest one to him, and scampering over to the burning vehicle. As he prepared the grenade, it quickly dawned on me his intentions. The screams of burning tank crewmen are a sound that no man should ever have to endure. Bobby scrambled up the raised bank and hopped onto the vehicle hull. Leaning as far as the flames would allow, dropping the potato masher into the open hatch. Instantly, the front of the tank was splashed in tracer bullets, which screamed and bounced in all directions, some even flicking down into the raised bank of the road. Bobby was now just a slumped mass of dusty black uniform, which was half propped on the burning hull, and over the panzer's gun mantlet.

I scrambled to my feet, wiping the tears from my grimy face.

'Fuck you' I roared, 'fuck you all!'

I turned and ran; hugging the raised bank and scuttled past our previous fighting positions. I didn't look back; the Americans could be on that position anytime now. They wouldn't give one SS soldier any quarter, so why take the chance? I just kept going, the raised road would take me into the Teutoburg, I knew that much, I had to get out of there, I didn't want to die, not today, not tomorrow, not for anyone, not for the fucking Fuhrer, not the Fatherland, no fucker. What have you got yourself into here Erik?

## PART 2

### 1.

I hadn't gone too far, when I started to run out of steam. My lungs ached as they tried to draw in the cold afternoon air, my legs felt like they weighed a tonne, my damp stocking feet were rubbing raw inside my boots. I was in the long ditch at the side of the raised road. The section I was in stretched off in almost a perfect straight line that reached far into the Teutoburg. Huge, thick trees marked the boundary of the road; there was no fear of me leaving the supposed sanctuary of the ditch anytime soon. Off to my right the sparsely planted tree trunks gave way to open farmland. Attempting to cross it in daylight was as good a suicidal. The Americans must have arrived on my previous position by now, to admire their handiwork.

I continued to blunder down the long ditch, cursing under my breath. How on earth was we supposed to stop the Americans with tanks that had no fucking fuel, no ammunition, where was our precious fucking Luftwaffe? Where the hell was our artillery? Why are we even fighting now the Russians are as good as in Berlin? Bobby's hometown had already been overrun; Berlin was not too far from there. I'd paid enough attention in school to know that. What was the Fuhrer expecting us to do without anything to do it with? Max would drum into us the importance of keeping the Americans at bay. If we surrendered, we would be handed over to the Russians, our mothers and sisters would become whores for the invader. Don't get me wrong, I was not in favour of testing the theory at that precise moment, but surely the madness must end soon? There couldn't be much left of Germany to capture.

What about after the war? All this talk of Jews, and our exploits in Russia. What will come of it? Would we all be held to account? Would all SS be sent to Siberia? I hadn't heard of any of these tales until recently, how the hell did I know what was going on in fucking Russia. Would they send me to Siberia? Mother would be heartbroken. All her sons lost to the war. Willi in France last year, we haven't heard anything from Manfred in Russia for months now, and now me. Was mother still at the house? I sure hoped she was safe, I hope she was not turfed out into the streets by the Americans to join those fleeing the fighting. Our cellar was strong; she must be living down there surely.

I wanted to go home.

Thoughts of my own preservation raced through my head. It was selfish I know, but all those who stood for what was good for Germany were now either dead or captured, with those of us remaining about to be branded criminals. The road started a long slow climb up into the hills. I was losing light as the early April day came to a close, and the close tree canopy either side of the road made it prematurely darker. As I crested what turned out to be a false horizon, I was met with a rather random and bizarre sight. Fallen trees. This would not be out of the ordinary in any forest, but these were lying across the road. Side by side. A road block perhaps? I'm no lumberjack by any stretch of the imagination, but whoever did the cutting clearly was not a man of the woods. Their handy work was poor. Either through lack of skill on the part of the woodsman, or had the skill but not the tools to do the job neatly. The bases of the trees on my side of the road were badly hacked, splintered in a very messy fashion. The cut trees were alternated with each other. One from my side of the road was felled, then the same on the other side. I had to climb out of the ditch and skirt through the woods to the right to avoid the huge cluster of branches, and few remaining leaves that hampered my progress. I considered walking on the road itself, but that would mean clambering over the trees trunks, some of which were very wide. I didn't have the energy for that.

Judging by the paleness of the trees innards, they had been cut recently. You can always tell how fresh wood is by how pale it was underneath the bark. This road block, there can be no other reason for it, was done recently, but by whom? Had we got units positioned in the hills around me? I wasn't sure to be relieved or scared at this prospect. Would they welcome me as an extra pair of hands, or treat me as a deserter? I stood still for a moment to catch my breath, scanning through the woods, trying to pick up signs of life. If there were troops occupying the area, their battlefield discipline was excellent. Besides the chopped down trees, there was nothing to give away human occupation. Way off in the distance, back towards Paderborn, there was the dull echo of tank fire. Someone still had some fight in them. Content I was alone at this time; I continued my climb towards Berlebeck.

It wasn't long before I'd crested the hill, and it began to slowly sweep downwards once again. I took the decision to walk on the road from there on, since trudging through the ditch, and fighting my way past the fallen trees had really sapped at my legs. Walking on the road felt great, the crunch of gravel under my boots echoed in the closed canopy that reached over the road from either side. Quietly confident the Americans were not screaming up behind me, I took the time to take stock of my current predicament. With the exception of two grenades, I was unarmed. Not much to fight with, but it's all I had. No food had been eaten for a while; the growling in my belly confirmed this. No water, my thirst was growing with each passing minute. It was getting cold, but my walking kept the cold at bay for the time being. I was a tired, smelly, dirty mess at that point, nothing a bowl of hot water wouldn't cure. I was confident that the good citizens of Berlebeck would help out this young soldier. They probably couldn't arm me with weapons, but a bite to eat, some coffee and a bath would be a gift from the gods.

As the last of the light faded, I could just make out the profile of buildings. No lights were to be seen, not even candlelight. I continued along the road until I'd passed the first small houses which were tucked into the trees. No people, no light, no livestock making a noise. I could hear the light trickling of a stream off to my right. With caution, I made my way towards the noise. It grew louder to a point where I was almost standing in it. Kneeling down, I cupped my hands to scoop myself a mouthful. It tasted okay to me, so I kept repeating the motion until I had my fill. Once content, I filled my water bottle. I was tempted to strip for a crude wash, but if I just ventured abit further into town, I might be able to get myself some better ablutions. I moved back onto the road and continued on. After a short time, it dawned on me that the small village was as good as deserted.

I made the decision to break into one of the houses. Spoilt for choice, I just chose the one nearest the road. I slowly picked my way over, the light as good as gone. My night vision really had its work cut out, since the overhead trees kept any ambient light out of the village. As I approached what appeared to be the front door, I could just make out the profile of a tractor, and some kind of plough in front of me. I carefully skirted around it to the left and made my way along the wall of the house. All its shutters were closed. I almost tripped over a set of wooden cellar trap doors that blocked my path. Carefully, I made my way around them, up the low steps to the front door. With caution, I took hold of the large, bulbous handle giving it a slow twist. The door was unlocked. The door creaked as I slowly pushed it open. I felt I should announce myself at the threshold before sneaking in, just in case I came across a heavily armed scared farmer.

'Hallo'

No answer.

'Hallo, anyone home?'

Nothing.

I straightened myself up, confident no trigger happy farmer was going to blast me as I walked through his home. I took care as I made my way down the corridor. As my night vision tried to adjust to the even less light inside the house, all appeared rather orderly. What features I could make out appeared to be where it they should be, no sign of a hasty departure. Ahead of me was what appeared to be a heavy curtain covering another doorway. I put my hands forward, touching the thick, rough material. To me, it had the rough texture of hessian, like sandbags. I put my hand through the left side of it and slowly swept my hand across to reveal what was behind. Cold steel pressed into the base of my skull. My stomach turned over.

'You need to be more careful whose' house you break into soldier.'

I stammered.

'Sorry Sir, tired, hungry, just looking for food.'

'What is your name soldier?' the voice behind me asked.

'Erik Sir' I gasped.

'Don't move Erik' whispered the voice, 'do you understand?'

I nodded frantically, the cold steel pressed against my head rattled on the rim of my helmet.
The pressure on the back of my head eased, followed shortly after by the closing of the front door. I was now trapped. I tried to control my shivering. But I dare not move. I heard the familiar striking of a

match, after a few seconds there was a soft glow behind me, which slowly got brighter.

'Turn around Erik.'

I cautiously turned around. In the soft glow of the lamp, I could see a man, in uniform holding a pistol. As I focused on the man before me, he appeared to be in German uniform, but no badges. Unshaven, scruffy haired. He moved towards me with an outstretched hand.

'Relax Erik; I'm Thomas' he grinned, 'just being careful when meeting new neighbours.'

Relief washed over me, I took his gesture, shaking his hand enthusiastically.

'Hello Thomas, fair enough, no problems.'

Thomas looked me over carefully.

'Why would an SS soldier be in Berlebeck on a night like this?' he enquired.

'My unit was destroyed at Schlangen; I had nowhere else to go.'

His eyes narrowed. 'The Americans are in Schlangen?'

I nodded, 'yes, tanks, but up until when we got hit with artillery, no sign of infantry.'

Thomas looked at me sternly, 'come with me'.

He then led me through the heavy dark material hanging over the door. It appeared to be double layered; my first attempt to see what was behind it would have failed since there was another sheet of it hanging from the other side of the doorway. He led me into what appeared to be the main communal area of the house, basic furnishings revealed themselves in the soft light given off by two oil lamps. I followed him through another doorway, no curtain this time, a door was fitted, but propped open with what looked like a large chunk of cut wood. Thomas's boots clattered on tiles, which led me to believe that we were entering the kitchen, the glow of the lamp Thomas was carrying confirmed this. The kitchen was a basic affair, large wood table and chairs dominated the space, with ground level units covering three sides of the room. The door that would lead out into the garden had more of the dark material covering it, as did the window above the sink and draining board. The glow of the lamp revealed a wooden door, which was closed flush along the right wall, Thomas opened it outwards and stepped through, and I followed him down some creaking wooden stairs into the basement. Let's just say, what I discovered in the basement was nothing short of bizarre.

Bearing in mind, the house I'd chosen looked pretty big in the poor light; this basement clearly covered the whole floor space of it. It was huge. As I stood at the bottom of the stairs, a large number of oil lamps allowed me to take in the scene around me. Off to the right side was row upon row of what could only be described as folding cot beds. Basic frames, with a canvas sheet held taught. All had blankets on, and some of them even had sleeping people on them. To the left of me was a crude sort of headquarters. Large map of Germany on the wall, to the right of it was a more detailed map of Paderborn and the surrounding area. Directly beneath the maps, I could make out the profile of someone sitting with their back to me. The figure had a set of head phones on, as I moved closer, I saw in front of him a large radio set, crackling away, with muffled dialogue coming through the headset. The sitting figure scribbled furiously on a piece of paper.

Further lo the left was a series of wooden constructs, which helped prop up a large number of weapons against the wall. The was a mixed bag of Platoon level weapons, Pistols, Rifles, Sub-machine guns, a couple of MG42, even a flamethrower.

Thomas caught my attention with a click of his fingers and waved me to him. As I stood with him, he gave the radio operator a nudge.

'Dennis, this is Erik, he was wandering like a stray by the house.'

I held out my hand, Dennis eyed me up and down before offering me his.

'Why would an SS soldier be wandering about here?' he directed the question at Thomas.

'Things have developed in Paderborn quicker than we anticipated. When is Dieter's team due back in?'

'In the early hours, they've still got some trees to cut' replied Dennis.

So there was someone out there. Allowing me to pass through unchallenged.

Thomas placed his hand on my shoulder.

'No point waiting for them idiots to get back, you might as well get some rest, you look like shit.'

I let out a boyish chuckle, 'thanks, I must admit, it's been a while since I've had some proper sleep.'

He led me over to a bed in the corner, 'here take mine, I'm on radio watch in a minute, Dennis has been glued to that thing for some time.'

'Thank you' I replied gratefully, 'thank you very much.'

He nodded, eyeing me up and down.

'You can get all that crap off before you get in my bed. We need you ready to talk first thing in the morning. Dieter will be very interested in any information you may have with regards to Paderborn.'

I feeling of dread washed through me, 'am I in trouble?'

Thomas grinned, 'no, you're not in trouble, we just need to know what the Americans are up to, that's all. Don't fret over it now; get all that crap off and get some sleep, okay?'

I nodded, Thomas walked away, giving Dennis a load of abuse, since it was clearly his turn to man the radio. I took my helmet off, it felt like an age since my hair saw the light of day. My belt kit came off without much trouble. I stripped down to my underwear, folding my clothing neatly, despite being filthy, and placing my equipment on top. I did not want to offend anyone with my equipment sprawled all over the place. As I lay on the cot bed, it felt like the most comfortable bed in the world. I pulled the blanket over me, giving me a feeling of isolation from the rest of the world.

## 2.

Hushed voices tuned in as I slowly opened my heavy eyelids. Tilting my head to the right, I slowly focused on a group of soldiers who were taking their equipment off and placing it on their cot beds. I leant further over; there was commotion and dialogue where the radio operator was stationed. As my vision improved, I could make out the profile of Thomas, whose body language was rather animated as he spoke to a larger built man. I couldn't make out his features, the oil lamps were placed in such a fashion, and I could only see his silhouette. I propped myself up on my elbows. I must have had the king of sleeps. I felt rather fresh. I just hoped I was not about to be marched out into the garden and shot because of my legendary snoring. I felt it only polite to quickly get dressed, and thank Thomas for his hospitality.

Fully dressed, helmet correctly wedged under my left armpit, I quickly ran my fingers through my hair before walking confidently over to Thomas. As I drew near, the conversation with the other man abruptly ended. I apologised for my intrusion, and thanked them for their lodgings. Thomas held up a hand to cut me short.

'Erik, this is Dieter, he's our commander and Director of Operations, Dieter, young Erik here was wandering like a stray cat outside the house last night. He felt it wise to break into our home, so is now under our charge.' Thomas gave me a wink.

I stood to attention, heels snapping together, about to raise the customary salute, when this huge hand of Dieter grabbed my right arm. I jumped out of my skin. Dieter's piercing glare was enough to tell me that he disapproved of such things.

'We don't do that kind of thing around here Erik, do you understand?'

I gulped loudly, 'yes Sir, my apologies.'

Dieter released his iron grip from my bicep, allowing the blood to flow again, his glare switched to Thomas.

'You and young Erik here meet me in the kitchen in a couple of minutes, okay?'

Thomas nodded, 'sure, coffee?'

Dieter grinned, well more of a sinister leer than a smile, 'coffee will be great; it's been a long night.'

With that, the huge imposing frame of Dieter moved over to what was apparently his bed, and stripped off his fighting gear. Minus his equipment, and stripped down to his undershirt, braces, trousers and boots, he still looked no smaller. Through his undershirt, it was clear to see he was in peak physical condition. I'm no nutritionist, but how could a man maintain such a physique with the lack of food around here? That reminded me, it had been a while since I'd eaten, my stomach groaned, hopefully I could fill it with sweet coffee, if nothing else.

Thomas led me upstairs into the kitchen. Daylight was slowly filling the room. The cloth material had been rolled up, allowing the outside world in. There was a soldier stood at the stove, playing chef, the coffee was on the go. A large pot on the stove was on the boil, I could make out the aroma of potatoes and vegetables. On the kitchen table was crockery, a large plate in the middle had large chunks of bread on it. Not entirely sure how fresh it was, but at that moment in time, who gave a shit? The chef turned around and acknowledged Thomas, who seized the opportunity to introduce me.

'Johann, this is Erik, found him last night sniffing around here. Another pair of hands to help out.'

Johann was heavily bearded, unkempt hair. Maybe he was one of the sleeping soldiers downstairs? In undershirt, trousers and boots, he looked me up and down before offering his hand.

'So this is the Waffen SS of today? How old are you boy?' he enquired.

I stood up straight, pushing my chest out somewhat, 'seventeen'.

He slowly offered his hand, shaking his head, 'so now we are sending children to fight, please don't take offence young Erik, I'm sure you have the fight of Germany in your heart.'

As I accepted his hand, 'yes Sir.'

He dismissed the 'Sir' with a casual wave of his other hand, 'no need for that 'Sir' shit with me boy, there's only one boss man around here, and it's that big ugly bastard running the show'.

'Get back to your stove woman, and fetch me my coffee', the huge frame of Dieter entered from the cellar, taking a seat at the table, gesturing me and Thomas to sit also. Johann rolled his eyes and got back to his chores.

Dieter stared at me for a while before opening any discussion. He was a menacing looking character, somewhat intimidating. If he was to brush his ash blonde hair, and shave off several days' worth of growth, he would be the poster boy for the Waffen SS. His piercing blue eyes complete the recruiting poster image in my head.

'Are you hungry Erik?' Dieter broke the silence.

'Yes Sir, it's been so long since I've eaten.'

His giant hand pushed the plate of bread in my direction, 'eat boy, it's not getting any fresher.'

I looked at Thomas for approval, who nodded towards the plate. I lost no time helping myself to the largest chunk of semi stale bread, and tucked right in. Delicious. Johann placed small metal cups of coffee in front of all three of us. He had made two jugs of coffee leaving one with us and taking the other with him back down into the cellar, leaving the pot of potato and vegetables to bubble away.

'What unit are you part of Erik?' began Dieter.

'I haven't been assigned to a unit yet. I was in the Senne, training when we got rounded up with our instructors and marched to Borchen.' I had to slow down my chewing to be heard properly, and to fight off the looming indigestion.

Dieter nodded,' that would explain why you have no cuff title.' Each SS division was awarded a cuff title, which let people know what division you belonged to. I'd yet to receive mine, given the circumstances, I doubt I ever would.

'Why Borchen?' Dieter continued.

I gulped down another lump of bread,' we were told the Americans were just south of Borchen, and were advancing on Paderborn.'

'Did they enter Borchen?'

'Yes, but we smashed them with panzerfausts and machine guns.'

Dieter grinned with an approving nod,' good boy Erik, but why are you now all the way out here?'

'We only had so much ammunition; our armour was also out of fuel and ammunition, so the Hauptsturmfurher in charge of us ordered us to withdraw.'

'Withdraw?' Dieter's eyes narrowed to a glare. 'To where may I ask?'

'We put in a few ambushes on our way back to Schlangen, we were told there would be reinforcements coming down through Kohlstadt to link up with us so we could counter attack.'

Dieter's clenched jaw, and huge clenched fists gave away the fact that he was not pleased, 'so the fucking mighty SS allowed the enemy to capture Paderborn, along with its road and rail network!'

I nodded, avoiding eye contact, 'yes Sir.'

' Why are you in Berlebeck?'

I looked up at him,' what was left of my unit was destroyed at Schlangen; American artillery smashed us badly, knocking out the two panzers in our position, burying my squad alive. I doubted the Americans would take pity on me, so I made my way up here.'

Dieter nodded, 'where are you from?'

'Paderborn.'

Dieter waved a dismissive hand, ''I know that boy, where were you born?'

'Paderborn.'

'What?' Dieter whispered leaning forward, a look of disbelief replacing his stern gaze.

'I'm from Paderborn, Sir', looking him square in the face, 'Bad Lippspringe.'

Dieter lurched back, which made me jump, he fumble for the cooker knob to turn off the hob, breakfast was ready. He stood up, his massive hand outstretched.

'Welcome to, shall we say, the Reichsfuhrer's plan B.'

I stood up to meet him, 'what do I need to do?'

Dieter grinned, 'first, eat breakfast, second, take all those fucking badges off.'

## 3.

Breakfast was nothing to write home about. It filled my belly, the bread more than made up for it. It may have been nearly stale, but it was nice to have bread in my diet. The coffee was okay, but then again, beggars couldn't be choosers.

I was sat at the kitchen table, with my breakfast knife, carefully picking away at the stitching on my tunic. Other soldiers were coming and going from the cellar, and out in the gardens around the house. They didn't give me a second glance, confidently going about their routine, whatever that was. Thomas emerged from the cellar and took his seat at the table once again. He was fully dressed, minus his tunic badges and helmet. He remained unshaven, but despite his dishevelled appearance, his MP40 which he placed on the table looked immaculate. Looking at his tunic, it was clear to see, he had been in the SS a while. The material was rather faded, yet the cloth beneath where his badges once were, was still its original field grey colour. Loose threads remained where the badges once were, indicating that he must have just ripped them off. The dark field grey patches on his right sleeve, indicated that he had been awarded 'Tank Kill' badges, and the horizontal strip across the wrist were his cuff title once sat. I had to ask.

'Thomas, what division was you?'

'Das Reich' I got wounded in France last year. Once my sick leave was up, they posted me to the Senne, teaching boys like you to kill tanks.'

'How did you end up here?'

'While at the Senne, I'd heard my division was as good as destroyed, trying to get out of France, and they were going to reassign me to the 'Totenkopf'. I though fuck that, there was no way I was going to Russia, so I took some leave, but never went back.'

'How did you avoid the Military Police?' I pushed.

'I just went about my own business, fully dressed, with a confident manner. People didn't give me a second glance. I was sat in a Beer Keller in Detmold, when I saw Dieter, and a couple of the guys sat across from me, one of them being Dennis. They waved me over, and it was clear they were all from different divisions. All in the same boat as me. None of us wanted to go back to our units, so we all got our heads together, agreeing that we still had to fight, but on our own terms. It was Dennis who told us about the Reichsfuhrers 'Werewolf' directive. He said he'd heard it when manning a radio shortly before. The directive wanted volunteers, with a rogue streak for adventure and trouble, but yet loyal to the Fatherland, to continue fighting the invader of our homeland. Away from conventional fighting units. So we thought here would be a good place to start.'

I was somewhat puzzled, 'what about Fuhrer directives?'

Thomas shrugged his shoulders, 'apparently he dismissed the idea as defeatism, claiming that an insurgency is admitting we have lost the conventional campaign. I'm not entirely sure we serve with the Fuhrers blessing right now, but we have a job to do. Harass and destroy the invader. You telling us about the Americans in Schlangen have certainly raised the stakes, let me tell you. That is why I introduced you to Dieter.'

It was now becoming clear, as a wave of dread washed through me. Deserter, now an insurgent. What was this war coming to? The rules of the game had certainly changed now, but the aim stayed the same, fight the invader.

'We've got alot to do today', Thomas snapping me out of my self pity,' the road block needs finishing off, before we get to work tonight.'

'Work tonight?' I frowned.

Thomas grunted, giving me a sly grin,' killing Americans Erik, killing Americans.'

My stomach turned over, there could be thousands of them in Paderborn by now, with more tanks and firepower than we could ever imagine.

Thomas could sense my uneasiness about the whole prospect,' not all of them mind, but sentries that wander too far, stuff like that.'

This sounded more like it, I quickly thought hard to get all the silly thoughts of mad, suicide charges at machine guns, tanks etc, out of my head. Taking out stragglers, and those who are sloppy in their personal security, I could deal with that, I suppose. I looked at my tunic, I hadn't made much progress with the badges, so if you can't beat them, join them. I picked at each one until I could get my finger underneath them, and ripped them off. Badges off, I pulled out as many of the loose threads I could find, and put my tunic on. I felt scruffy, something I was not used to at all. Our instructors would be all over us, if we had so much a hair out of place. This carefree abandon on personal appearance here was something I would have to get used to. I could hear commotion in the cellar as multiple pairs of boots could be heard clattering up the stairs. It appeared that all the soldiers that were either sleeping or removing their kit earlier this morning were gathering in the kitchen. I felt above my station being sat at the table, and attempted to give up my seat for one of the more seasoned guys. A firm hand on my shoulders and a friendly 'relax' was muttered as I stayed fixed in the seat. Dieter was the last to squeeze through the cellar door, picking his way through the guys, who struggled to find a spot in the now rather crowded kitchen. I carefully peered around the room, all were unshaven, scruffy haired, some had scars on their faces, all their tunics were minus their relevant badges, yet their weapons, like Thomas', were clean and ready to go. Dieter raised a huge hand, calling for hush.

'Main effort today guys, getting the road block finished. Thomas, your team will take care of that, whilst my lot will go take a look at the Americans in Schlangen. Information gratefully received from young Erik here.'

I felt like a right idiot, sat at the table, with all these combat veterans looking at me. Dieter continued.

'It appears that we have friendly forces coming down through Kohlstadt anytime soon, to take on the Americans. So my guys, we must ensure that if they do turn up whilst we are there, we are not caught in the middle. We will see what they are up to, and then we can go to work tonight on those bastards who feel they can relax in our back yard. We will also act as early warning should the enemy decide to move up towards the road block.'

Dieter then looked at Dennis,' are the radios good to go?'

'Yes', Dennis nodded,' battery life could be better, but should be okay for today.'

'Remember guys' ,Dieter continued, 'today is about road block building and information gathering, if the shooting starts, we are to get away, and pick another fight later on, okay?'

Everyone nodded.

'Right then, get your shit sorted, and be outside in the next five minutes, less Dennis and Felix, they will monitor the radio here, and make sure we have no more nosey visitors.' To emphasise this, Dieter leered at me. I felt rather uncomfortable.

The clattering of kitchen chairs and boots reigned as everyone went about their business. A hand on my right shoulder made me jump.

'You will replace Felix in my team today okay?' Thomas explained.

'Sure' I was pleased to be on the road block task, I wasn't confident about heading back to Schlangen any time soon. Thomas instructed me to take an MP40 from the cellar, half a dozen magazines, a grenade, and an axe for which would have a lot of use today. Before long, I was stood outside the front of the house, it was rather chilly, but I chose to wear my smock over my tunic, just to keep the wind off. It did feel rather odd not to wear a helmet, almost naked even, but since no one else was wearing one, why draw attention to myself?

Dieter led his team off first, whilst our team stood around a little while longer, smoking cigarettes, and finishing off their coffees, all very relaxed and civilised. Thomas took this opportunity to introduce me to the rest of his team. Stood before us was Johann, whom I'd just met whilst making breakfast, he no longer looked like the scullery maid, but very much a soldier. Unshaven, and rather dishevelled, but looked like he could cause alot of trouble at a moment's notice. Then we had Viktor, who once again looked like the poster image you'd expect of the German Army. He was our radioman for the task, and then I was introduced to Gerhard. Short, stocky and powerful, once again, with the limited food resources around here, how did he manage to keep in such fine shape? Once all the hand shaking and shoulder slapping had finished, cigarettes were stamped out, we then set off on task. The maintenance of the roadblock.

We patrolled out of Berlebeck back the way I had travelled the night before. The early April light had managed to penetrate the thick, spindly branches that reached across the main road. Thomas took the lead, with Viktor, Gerhard, and Johann fallen in behind respectively. I played it safe and loitered at the rear, no one appeared to mind, after all, we were not on a fighting patrol, at least I hope we wasn't. We slowly made our way up the long winding road towards the top of the ridgeline I had climbed. The trickling stream to our left sat in a shallow gorge ran parallel with the raised bank that held up the road. Daylight allowed me to tune into the environment alot better. The whole ridgeline that formed part of the Teutoburg Wald was coated in thick, ancient trees, which would during full blossom, block out a lot of daylight, giving you a feel of fighting at dawn or dusk, whatever time of day you happened to be doing so. Winter had stripped them of their leaves, and I could make out early signs of new life beginning to sprout from them. The gradient in which we ascended began to really become more severe. Up on the skyline, I could just make out the last two of Dieter's team cresting it. Thomas kept the pace slow and steady, but it still didn't stop us from puffing and panting. I was grateful to not be wearing a helmet at this stage, since sweat was running freely down my temples, gathering underneath my chin, which I would wipe away with the cuff of my smock. I could have done without the smock for that matter, I was the only one wearing one, but back at the house, it was rather cold outside, stood around ready to go.

Just short of the summit, Thomas waved us over to the side of the road, and indicated for us all to close up.

'We will give Dieter and his guys' abit of a lead before we move over and get to work. If the Americans have any surprises for us, Dieter will be the first to know about it.'

Made sense to me.

The other lads lost no time getting their tobacco out, and savouring every moment of their rest time. Judging by their body language, they knew there were no Americans around here. This was their neighbourhood, nice and safe. Gerhard broke the silence.

'Relax boy, the Americans are not fans of the Wald. We learned that very quickly in the Ardennes. Felix said the same about their exploits in the Hurtgen. The Americans are only happy if they can fight on a road. Their infantry are not ones for the forest. Relax.'

I nodded at Gerhard's' claim, I had heard of those horrific winter battles in the forests. Both us and the Americans paid dearly for them. But for some reason, we would trade space for time and withdraw to reset our frontline. Why? If we were as good as we claimed in fighting in the forest, why did we pull back? I already knew the answer to this, American firepower, and the Russians. What have you got yourself into here Erik?

Once their cigarettes were finished we got to our feet, adjusted our loads, and trudged on. Over the ridgeline, the road meandered slowly down to where the trees were laying across the road. We followed Thomas over to a spot near a rather large tree. He instructed us to strip down to just undershirts, but keep our weapons slung on us at all times. Once ready, MP40 slung, with axe in hand, we went to work. Thomas tasked Gerhard and me to tidy up the fallen trees across the road, whilst Viktor and Johann dealt with the trees on the flanks. Thomas would sit with the radio, like a Foreman on a work site.

Gerhard clambered onto the first of the huge trees. Reaching down to help me up. Once up on the logs, we went to work, chopping away any branches that were sticking up. Gerhard explained the method to the madness.

'We want the American tanks not to see the roadblock until they crest the false horizon just before the logs. They are then committed, and therefore stuck in a traffic jam, you see?'

I did. Made perfect sense to me. If they spot it early, they could detour around it, making all the work for nothing. We made steady progress, dealing with each log in turn. Once complete, Gerhard inspected our work, putting the finishing touches to that part of our task. He appeared satisfied.

'Right then, we now need mud.' He stated.

We clambered off the log nearest the false crest. We ventured over to the side of the road, Gerhard peering in the ditch. He jumped in with both feet, sinking almost knee deep in the dark sludge that coated the bottom. He dug is hands into the mire, with all the enthusiasm of a toddler who is left unattended in the garden. He revealed his hands to me, all covered in mud and leaf litter.

'Perfect!' he beamed, 'don't be shy boy, get your arse in here and get stuck in.'

I copied him. Hands now plastered in mud and leaf litter, we scrambled out of the ditch, and watched what Gerhard had in mind. He covered the bare, white splinter timber with the stuff. The penny dropped, as Gerhard informed me why.

'Their tank commanders will see the splintered ends first, which could cause them concern. Cover them in mud, and they have nothing to worry about until they get up here.' He gave me a mischievous wink.

I went to task with enthusiasm. It can be safely said, this was the first time in my short military career that someone actually explained the reasons why certain things were done. On the Senne, most of the time, our instructors would scream at us what we had to do, and God help any of us if we so much had the inclination to ask why. I now knew why we removed the up facing branches, and why we covered the white splintered ends in mud. I enjoyed this type of work, mainly because there was a bloody reason to it. The aim of the roadblock was to prevent their tanks rolling down into Berlebeck. That would not be good for me, if I was tucked up in bed after working all night.

It took some time to coat the broken ends of the logs in mud, but we slowly got there. Thomas called a coffee break, and as a good foreman, he had a flask of coffee to share amongst us. His muddy, sweaty workforce gathered before him. Coffee and cigarettes went around the group with a laugh and a jeer. I didn't smoke, so I just sat still and enjoyed the coffee as it was passed around.

In what appeared to be just a matter of minutes, Thomas jokingly called us all a bunch of lazy bastards, and told us to get back to work. We got to our feet, gathered our tools, and got on with it. Gerhard and I were still plastering trees in mud, and the other guys were felling them. Throughout the morning, I'd heard the creaking and splintering of trees as they crashed and thudded to the ground around us. My main effort at this stage still involved handfuls of leaf litter and mud, but this time we had to cover the broken tree stumps that remained in place. We had to be diligent so we didn't give away our intentions to eagle eyed American tank commanders. An exposed broken stump or tree limb could mean that man had been here recently, and could mean an ambush, so we had to cover our handy work. Before long, the stumps were dealt with. Feeling rather proud of myself, I admired what we had achieved that morning. The splintering crash of a tree falling brought my attention as to what the other guys were up to. Gerhard led me carefully up to where the other pair was working. A little way in from the road they had dropped every other tree in a long line of about a dozen. Then in the row behind, going alongside the roadblock they had dropped the alternate tree in the line. I was out of my depth to even fathom the method to this madness, but Gerhard read my frown, and quickly educated me.

'Picture the scene,' he beamed with enthusiasm, his hands out in front of him. He framed the guys working with his thumbs and forefingers, like a movie director. 'The American tanks encounter the roadblock, and try to skirt around it. They end up exposing the sides of their vehicles to our panzerfausts, and when they try to get through the gap in the trees, they either 'belly out' on the tree stump, or end up stuck straddling the fallen tree. Any sudden steering and they lose a track.'

Pure genius! Remind me again why we withdrew from the forests in the west. Oh yeah, that's right. Trading space for time.

Gerhard and I informed Johann and Viktor we would get to work on the other side. Copying what they were up to. We made our way over and got to work. I don't mind admitting that I preferred playing with the mud. Cutting them trees was bloody hard work. My technique was all wrong. Gerhard, a far more seasoned woodsman made it look easy, the bastard. Fair play to him, he had the patience of a saint as he watched this clown with an axe try and chop a bloody tree down. In my defence, these trees were centuries old, and bloody wide. He would laugh his arse off as I sweated and cursed nature, and all those who embraced it. After several tutorials from Gerhard, I started to get the hang of it. He was taking down nearly three trees to every one of mine. After a while, he'd had enough of me nearly breaking the axe, and told me to go back to mud duties, covering the stumps, and splintered ends of the fallen. Now that was my type of task.

Before long, we had three rows of trees and stumps covered in mud. Thirty six trees in total. My hands burned with calluses' from my poor chopping technique, I could only inspect them once I'd washed the mud off. Gerhard, although rather sweaty, still looked fairly fresh. I had to ask.

'Gerhard, where are you from?'

'Bavaria' he chuckled.

Say no more. Probably born with an axe in his hand.

'Shall we help our comrades fling mud at their trees?' It was a rhetorical question I'm sure, since he was already making his way over to the other pair. I followed him, far be it for me to take a coffee break whilst the others were still working.

With the exception of Thomas, who manned the radio, it was all hands to the pump, getting the remaining trees and stumps coated in mud. We were starting to lose light, so we had to get a move on. As we finished off the last stumps, Thomas wandered down, weapon slung behind his back, hands in pockets.

'Dieter's team is on its way back.' He informed us.' Hopefully, he can tell us what's going on in Schlangen.'

Content our work was done; we made our way back up to where we had left all our gear and the radio. The inactivity started to give me a chill as my sweat began to dry, so I got myself dressed. My smock was now a welcome addition, since a brisk breeze was now blowing over the ridgeline. In the fading light, we relaxed, smoked, chatted away about the usual shit soldiers talk about. Beer, women, the war, the Russians, the Americans, even the British. As the conversation became more candid, it was evident that everyone was trying their hardest to not talk about family and home. Homesickness overwhelmed me. I tried my hardest not to let it show, I'm sure some of the guys had their own fears as to the whereabouts and safety of their loved ones. It paid to be young in these instances. I was single, I had a fair idea that mother was okay. I had no wife or children to worry about. I didn't have to fear for my wife and daughters safety should they fall prey to the appetites of the invaders. Judging by the age range of all those around be, they had all this to contend with, and fight as well. What have you got yourself into here Erik?

The conversations had pretty much run their course, and we just sat there, deep in our own thoughts. The wind started to cut through our group, making it all the more colder as we sat up on the ridge line. I heard movement down at the roadblock, snapping of twigs, and the crunch of leaf litter. Dieter appeared, then one by one, the rest of his team. As they drew near, we could see steam coming off of them. All were glazed in a fine shine of sweat. Not too sure if it was the climb that made them perspire, or the pace Dieter had set, or the sheer fright of seeing so many Americans in Schlangen. We would soon find out.

'Not as much traffic down there as we originally thought', Dieter stated as he carefully laid his weapons at his feet. 'A few tanks, not too much infantry. We tried to see if they had occupied any of the houses, but there was nothing to indicate such a move.'

Thomas led Dieter away back down towards the roadblock, taking him on a tour of what we had achieved during their absence. The remainder of his team remained, smoking cigarettes, pulling their collars up to fend off the chilled, brisk air as it whipped between us. I didn't know these men, and thought better of being rather bold and introducing myself. A sudden hand on my shoulder made me flinch, my head snapped to the left seeing Gerhard's muddy paw attached to me, a beaming smile on his tired, unshaven face.

'Gentlemen, have you met our latest recruit? This is Erik, he has been a great help in building the road block you see before you.'

I gave a courteous nod in their direction. They nodded in return; their cigarettes were their primary concern, their shoulders hunched to fend off the cold second. Gerhard continued, introducing them each in turn, pointing at them in turn, from left to right.

'Anton, Konrad, Lars, and this handsome devil is Otto.'

The man introduced as Otto looked at the floor, shaking his head.

'Gerhard, you should be in the circus, not the SS.'

Gerhard gave an enthusiastic nod, 'once this war is over, that is my next career move. I think I would make a great lion tamer.'

This caused our little group to stifle a chuckle in the brisk wind that was picking up. Thomas and Dieter returned from their inspection of the road block. Dieter spoke as he gathered up his weapons.

'It starts right here tonight gentlemen.'

We all just looked at him, I was trying my hardest not to shiver, not too sure if it was the cold, or the pre match nerves once again. Dieter continued.

'We waste darkness by going back to the house at this time. My team plus young Erik here will be going to pick a fight tonight. The remainder of you will be here ready to assist if needs be, or to help us extract out of any mischief should it get too much for us, you never know with these Americans, one minute they are playing cards, the next they are unleashing hell on you before you have time to shit yourself. Well, it changes tonight, as of now, they will not enjoy a conquerors sleep, and they will once again fear the darkness.'

I peered around the group, their whole demeanour had changed, they no longer hunched their shoulders against the cold. They now stood almost at attention, both hands on their personal weapons, pushing their chests out as they took deep breaths. The cheery banter had now vanished for the night, a menacing leer was written across their faces.

Dieter scanned all of our faces, as it grew darker, his huge frame appeared all the more menacing, with a slow nodding head, he appeared to approve.

'They will fear the darkness.'

## 4.

Dieter took the lead. Otto, Konrad, Lars, and Anton fell in behind respectively. The new kid followed on once again at the rear. As I followed them down towards the right side of the roadblock, I peered around towards the other guys staying behind. I felt very much out of my comfort zone, I'd grown used to their company, especially Gerhard's'. Thomas gave me an approving nod, Gerhard a thumbs up; the others were too busy with cigarettes and taking a piss against a tree to wave me off. I turned back to my new patrol members as they picked their way through the mud and leaf litter. I carefully navigated my way around, following the path of the other guys, and before long we were on the actual road, heading downhill towards Schlangen and the Americans.

The approach to Schlangen appeared to take a very long time. It was as good as dark now. Dieter led at a steady, deliberate pace. Halting us now and then. During the halts, I strained to detect the sound of armoured vehicles, even perhaps foreign voices. All we could hear at this time was the wind rushing across the road which in turn caused the trees leaning over to sway under its force. No sign of enemy at this time. As we made progress, I slowly began to see the profile of buildings and the like in the distance. Dieter led us into the ditch which ran parallel on the right side. When I escaped from the artillery attack the other day, I had kept myself in the ditch on the other side of the road. The whole area appeared rather strange to me, since the circumstances of me being there had changed rather dramatically. I couldn't help but feel a sense of pride building up inside me. I was running for my life just the other day, now I was back to fight for Fuhrer and Fatherland.

After what felt like forever, we got to the outskirts of Schlangen. The rooftops of the town peered over the trees that, up until that point had almost hidden them from view. Across the road, out in the open field, I could just make out the burnt out hulks of the halftrack and the two panzers that occupied our last position. We continued straight ahead, into the first gardens, and the road slowly veered away from us to the left. The road which marked the front of my last position. The patrol pace was now painfully slow, as we picked our way around the chicken coops and wire strand fences. The odd chicken got rather excited as we passed by, which made me all the more nervous. The last thing we needed was a fucking chicken giving us away to the enemy. Perhaps we could steal one later for some meat in our vague and boring diet of vegetables and potatoes.

We came alongside one of the first wooden out buildings. We kept our eyes peeled should anyone be following us. I peered up at Dieter. His dark profile looked confident as he leaned out from our hiding place. This didn't surprise me. He'd probably already patrolled through here earlier today. No enemy sighted. With a faint snap of his fingers, he waved us forward. We continued with caution as we picked our way between the fences and various sized buildings as we ventured further into Schlangen. I was expecting it to be heaving with enemy forces, but it was quiet as you could imagine a sleepy little village. The odd cluck of a chicken, bushes and spindly trees fluttering in the chilling wind was all I could make out. No enemy sighted.

An abrupt and uncontrolled cough up front caused us all to stop in our tracks. Dieter waved us all down into cover with his huge hand. We slowly pushed away from the house we had knelt alongside and carefully took up positions behind a rickety wooden fence. I didn't have much faith in the fence stopping any bullets if the shooting started, but it beat kneeling on the doorstep of someone's home. I peered over the fence, trying to see around the corner where the supposed cough had originated. Nothing. I felt movement to my right. The rest of the team had begun crawling along the fence line. I followed them. We must have been in a cattle pen of some sorts, it smelt vile. We must have crawled for maybe fifty metres or so when those up front stopped. I wasn't paying attention and got a faceful of hobnailed boot smeared in cow shit. Great. The darkened grinning face of Anton welcomed me as I looked up. Arsehole. With my forearms, I propped myself up. I could see Dieter at a crouch looking over the fence. Keeping his profile low, he beckoned us to look where he was looking.

Before us sat one of their tanks. In the gloom, I wasn't sure what type it was, but my money was on a Sherman. It sat about thirty meters from where we were. The building to the left of it was occupied by someone. The faint glow of candlelight could just be made out. Shadows of people could just be made out as the flame flickered. As the wind blew, there was a dull clatter of metal to metal contact on or around the tank. As my eyes accustomed to what I was focused on, it became apparent the tank was draped in some kind of sheeting. Its main gun pointed skywards, causing this sheeting to peak like a large tent of sorts. This tank was not ready for action, that was for certain, but I couldn't be sure of the whereabouts of its crew. Dieter and the others remained motionless for some time. We couldn't do anything daring until we knew where all the fucking crew were. The cold was really starting to get to me at this point. What didn't help was the fact that someone was in the house keeping warm. Enemy soldiers? Civilians? We just didn't know at that point.

From the rear right of the tank as we looked at it, a lone figure appeared. This caused my heart to race. This was probably the closest I'd come to seeing an American, with the exception of the one manning their machine gun back in Borchen. My look at him was very brief, since I felt he was about to obliterate me with that huge machine gun. The lone figured was merely a silhouette. I couldn't make out any features. It walked slowly alongside the tank until he was at the front right corner. The features became a little clearer. This figure was not wearing a helmet; I struggled to make out if it had a weapon of any kind. The lone figure peered towards the building with the light inside. The penny dropped. The rest of them are in there. He's on sentry duty. The figure made his way towards the dimly lit building. As he drew up to the shutters, I could just make out him speaking to someone. There was a flicker of a spark, then another. He was getting a cigarette.

I noticed movement to my right. My stomach turned over as I saw Dieter strolling very casually towards the tank. How the fuck did he get over the fence so quietly? I snapped my head to the remainder. They appeared just as animated and concerned as I.

'Was the hell is he doing?' I whispered to Anton, through gritted teeth.

'I have no idea,' he replied, shaking his head frantically, 'it's going to get real interesting around here in a minute.'

Dieter continued his leisurely stroll towards the tank, as if he was in no rush. My heart was racing; I came over all sweaty very quickly. I dare not take my eyes from the sentry talking in between the window shutters. Like a blind man, I felt my way around my weapons, and made sure I had the fresh magazines close to hand. Pre battle nerves could give a man a heart attack, I'm sure of it. I couldn't remember if I had cocked the weapon, putting a round into the breach. For heaven's sake Erik, always be ready to fight! Dieter made it to the tank and lurked around the right side as we were looking at it. The sentry continued to chat and giggle with whoever was in the window. The sentry's face illuminated brightly as he took a drag, I could just make out the profile of whom he was talking to, not much else as the light faded. Whatever Dieter had in mind better be quick. He knelt down next to the tracks; I could just make out his silhouette as it moved slowly and deliberately. Our sentry had now finished his conversation with his friend and backed away from the window. Dieter stood up and walked slowly towards the backing figure. The sentry spun around, aware someone else was there. There was that strange pause, as if he couldn't tell who it was. There Dieter was stood face to face with this sentry. Dieter flicked an arm up, with a loud snap, a spark of light shot the sentry in the face. His face shattered in a burst of red mist, his body dropping like liquid to his knees where it remained propped up against the front belly plate of his tank.

The bullet Dieter had fired instantly ploughed through his opponents' face, out the back of his skull and splintered one of the window shutters with a loud pop. Chickens in their coops got all excited clucking their heads off, which sounded very loud in the cold, still air. There was muffled commotion in the room as Dieter casually walked over to the left side of the window. There was the dull crash of furniture in the room as the tank crew got their act together. Me and other guys got our weapons up on top of the fence ready to fight. Dieter, with all the time in the world, prepared one of his grenades and sent it through, between the shutters. A squeal of panic echoed around the courtyard as it became apparent the tank crew was being ambushed. A huge thud instantly followed, causing the whole house to ripple with its concussion and echo. The stricken crew stumbled out of the front door, hands on their ears, half undressed straight into the killing zone of Dieter. Dieter dropped to one knee, taking deliberate shots with his pistol into the chest and faces of the grenade survivors. They piled up on top of each other as Dieter dispatched them as they came across the threshold, their bodies almost blocking the doorway. As the echoed died away, the sound of this short and very violent action was replaced by barking dogs, foreign voices shouting in the neighbouring streets. We had to get out of here now, right fucking now.

Dieter casually walked away to the left, giving us a wave to follow him. We kept low as we scampered back along the fence line to where we had entered the field. Dieter continued on without so much as looking behind to see if we were following. We fell in behind him as we made our way back the way we had come earlier in the evening. Me being at the rear of the column again, I spent more time walking backwards, convinced the Americans were chasing us up, armed with dogs. The barking had reached a crescendo, the voices slowly faded away. I don't think they were following us up. Thank heavens for that. We reached the raised road and quickly got into the ditch on the left, and increased the pace back towards the roadblock. I was sweating like a maniac, but I didn't mind one bit, as long as we were putting distance between us and the Americans.

Before long, after a real lick of a marching pace, we began to ascend the hill that took us up to the roadblock. Our handy work earlier that day had really paid off, it wasn't until we crested the false horizon did we come across the fallen trees Gerhard and I had prepared. We carefully picked our way around the branches and brush on the left side and we could slowly make out the profile of Thomas' team. There was a flurry of handshakes, shoulder slapping, and small talk before we all fell into column with Thomas and Dieter taking the lead back down the other side to the house. As we slowly trudged down the hill, exhaustion was starting to get the better of me. I welcomed the coming sleep. It had been a very long day. Despite the distance we had put between us and any potential pursuers, I couldn't help but keep looking behind us for any sign of the enemy. Perhaps the Americans were scared of fighting in the forests, fighting in the dark even. I was grateful that, by the looks of things they had chosen not to follow up. I needed sleep.

We had reached the house; all the windows were blacked out as expected. It was only just this time last night that I thought the place was unoccupied. How wrong I was. Concealed in the vast belly of the large, unassuming house were some heavily armed men, hell bent on causing trouble. That was evident, make no mistake. Our column slowly clambered through the doorway that led us straight into the kitchen. Soft lighting flicked in and out of sight as we kept the blackout curtain in place across the threshold. The kitchen was rather crowded by the time we had all got in. The aroma of cooking and coffee was unmistakable. More semi stale chunks of dark bread sat in a bowl in the centre of the table. Various weapons lay strewn all over the table as well. As I took in the view, the demonic glares at the start of the night were now gone, it was cigarettes and smiles all round, with the exception of Dieter who kept his devil mask on.

'Settle down, Felix, get that coffee dished out.' He demanded.

The commotion died down as grateful men thanked Felix as he distributed the sweet liquid into various cups and glasses found in the cupboards. Once everyone was dealt with, Dieter raised a hand for order.

'Just so we are all in the picture, especially Thomas' team who had the rather unglamorous job tonight of manning the roadblock, let's talk about what we have learned and achieved tonight.' He paused to take a sip of his own coffee. The long, closed eyes as he took in the coffee gave away the fact that he been looking forward to it for a while. He then continued.

'The Americans are already of the impression that the war is won, covering their vehicles and sleeping in the houses. This reassures me that they are not ready for action, and this will be our advantage.'

Nods all around the room acknowledged Dieters statement.

'Tonight however', he continued, 'we have changed their way of thinking I'm sure.'

'What did you see?' asked Thomas, full of anticipation. Dieter continued.

'We didn't venture too far into town tonight; we must be patient and pick our fights carefully. We encountered one of their tanks covered in a sheet, a lone sentry wandering about smoking, whilst his comrades rested in the house close by. We eliminated the crew, but we didn't take the time to disable their vehicle somehow.'

As I scanned the room, the menacing grins had returned. Me personally, I wasn't happy about the patrol at all, I was shit scared of getting ambushed or worse, captured. Dieter snapped me out of my self pity.

'We quickly withdrew, and the enemy did not chase us. You see men; they are scared of the dark and the Wald. They will be easy prey, mark my words.'

The room slowly filled with murmuring of agreement, shoulder slapping, cigarettes being lit, Dieter called for order.

'Time to rest, get some food, some more coffee, we have more work and planning to do tomorrow. Thomas' team will be on this next operation. We have plenty of panzerfaust in the cellar; I plan for us to start killing their tanks from now on.'

With that, everyone started getting up, gathering their coffee and weapons and making their way down into the cellar. It was easier for me to stay put until the kitchen had cleared. After a while, all who remained was Gerhard and I. Gerhard frowned at me.

'How did you deal with this tank crew? I didn't hear any gun fire.'

'Dieter killed them' I explained, 'he shot the sentry in the face with his pistol and put a grenade into the house. He killed the remainder as they attempted to escape the grenade.'

Gerhard grinned, not a menacing leer, but was clearly impressed.

'Not bad, not bad at all, they will be shitting themselves down there.' He indicated towards the direction of Schlangen.

I agreed, but I wasn't any less scared. Dieter scared me more than ever now. You always get a fair idea of those who talk the talk, and those who just blow a lot of hot air. Dieter looked the part, and had now confirmed to me that he was the part. I was still overwhelmed by his lack of personal safety as he calmly went about killing the tank crew. Makes you wonder why he took the rest of us at all. This guy was dangerous, and not just to the Americans either.

'Get some rest boy.' Gerhard piped up, 'unless you want to eat some of this boiled shit.' He lifted a ladle of boiled potato and vegetables out of the pan to get his point across. No thank you.

I took my leave and my gear down into the cellar. There was already the hum of snoring as I adjusted my vision to the dull lamps that let off a warm glow. Thomas and Dieter were talking in hushed voices as they pointed to the map of Paderborn on the wall. This was not a conversation I was interested in at that point, and went in search of an empty cot bed. I found one with not too much trouble, but quickly counted the remaining empty ones to ensure I wasn't about to sleep in someone else's'. The maths added up, and I confidently stowed my gear and weapons underneath it. It creaked as I carefully laid down, pulling the blanket up over my face. What a day.

# 5.

I woke with a start. Weapons being cocked. I sat bolt upright, only to be greeted by Otto, stripping his weapon down, placing the components on the cot bed next to him. A wave of relief washed over me as I lay back down. To be caught by the Americans down here would have only ended one way, and not in our favour. I rubbed the sleep from my eyes, focusing on the ceiling, not for anything in particular, it was just the easiest thing to look at, in my sleep drunken state.

'Erik, remind me never to have you in my ambush party.' Otto stated.

I peered up at him with a frown, not too sure how to respond.

Otto shook his head, 'your fucking snoring keeps the Eastern Front awake you noisy bastard.'

'Sorry' was all I could muster. It wasn't the first time my snoring brought a verbal reprimand to my ears first thing in the morning. In the Senne, it wasn't uncommon for our instructors to come crashing into our barrack block for roll call, and find half the troop's boots around my bed where they had attempted to silence me in the darkness.

I eased myself up into the sitting position, and took in the scene around me. Some beds were empty, but most were still filled with their occupants. Cigarettes glowed as those who had no real reason to get up yet just stayed put, with their hands behind their heads. The light grey smoke column drifting upwards, in various shapes. Some had even mastered blowing smoke rings. I wasn't a smoker, but it did fascinate me how they managed to do it. I flung my legs over the side and carefully slid my stocking feet into my boots. I ran my fingers through my hair, which was getting tougher by the day. I couldn't remember the last time I'd had a bath or shower. No one complained how I smelt, that was a bonus I suppose, but my snoring did me no favours, that were for sure.

'Tell you what', Otto piped up, a cigarette dangling between his lips as he wiped over the stripped down weapon before him, 'fetch me a coffee, and I will try my hardest to forgive you.'

I nodded, seemed like a fair trade, 'ok'.

I got to my feet, and carefully picked my way towards the stairs. The light from the kitchen told be the blackout curtains had been removed, daylight lit the room. I clumsily made my way up into the kitchen. I was greeted by the sight of Thomas and Dieter, sat at the table, pouring over a map, both armed with a pencil.

'Good morning', I smiled.

They stopped talking, looked me up and down, and then went back to talking to cach other.

Charming.

I spotted the coffee pot on the stove and made my way over, grabbing two tin cups as I went. They had just recently been used, but I wasn't too worried about that, I just wanted to quickly get them filled and get out of there. Dieter and Thomas looked like they had more trouble planned for us, my stomach tightening with the anticipation. Cups filled, a generous helping of sugar in them, I made my way carefully back into the cellar.

Otto had finished cleaning his weapon, and was lying back on his bed enjoying another cigarette. He sat bolt upright when I offered him one of the cups, carefully taking it from me with both hands.

'Thank you, young man.' Glad somebody around here was in the mood to be sociable.

We drank in silence; I was never much good at small talk. Once I'd finished my cup, I looked down at my own gear, feeling that I should maybe clean it or something. I picked up the MP40, removed the magazine, and then ensured there wasn't a round in the breach. There wasn't. That would have meant last night I could have wasted precious seconds cocking it before contributing to the fight. Not that there was any requirement, Dieter had killed the tank crew before I could take in what had just happened before me. With the weapon now stripped down to its basic component parts, I wiped it down with a cloth that Otto offered me, since he guessed I would need it. Once done, I took my time to inspect it for rust, I could not see any, and whoever owned this particular weapon before had taken great care of it. Once content the thing would work when I need it to, I reassembled it back together ensuring the firing mechanism worked correctly before replacing the magazine back into its housing. Done. I would only cock the weapon prior to going out on another operation, which I'm sure, wasn't too far away.

Otto nodded his approval, and gave off a rather large fart as he lay back down. Chuckles could be heard from various corners of the cellar, and the odd muttering of 'dirty bastard' from underneath various blankets. I then checked over my fighting gear, my grenades appeared to remain serviceable, and my belt kit was in an acceptable state for the company I was in. I doubt it would have passed muster in the Senne, but them days were well and truly gone by all accounts.

Heavy feet thudded down the stairs. Dieter peered over the hand rail.

'Get up you lazy bastards; we've got work to do.'

Blankets stirred more farts and coughs echoed around the now foul smelling room. One by one, the blankets gave up whoever they were hiding from the world, and the cellar began to come to life once more. I felt I should get out of their way, so I gathered up my gear and weapons, and made my way upstairs. As I took the first rung of the wooden staircase, I noticed Gerhard on radio watch. I caught his attention with a casual wave; he gave me a wink and thumbs up, and then began to scribble furiously as a muffled voice babbled away in the headset.

Trying to seek refuge in the kitchen wasn't a good idea either, since troops tend to want coffee and food of some description first thing, so I made my way out into the garden to avoid the people traffic. As I stood outside in the crisp April air, it was apparent, that with the exception of some soldiers occupying the house, the remainder of Berlebeck was almost untouched by the war. I moved away from the side of the house towards the road, the commotion of people and furniture faded somewhat, I tried to detect any other life in the village. I saw some chimneys giving away the fact that there were people cooking or trying to keep warm, but other than that, there were no other people to be seen.

I pulled my smock tighter around me and made my way back to the kitchen door. There was now just the hum of conversation coming from the kitchen, I made my way slowly back in. It was rather crowded at that point, but everyone appeared dressed and with coffee. Dieter and Thomas stood by the stove, poised to address us all. With standing room only, I managed to find a spot to place myself. Dieter called for quiet.

'Right guys, the plan for today is to get the roadblock finished off, by that I mean fighting positions, and this evening we are going back into town to see what we can do.'

He paused for it to sink in.

'We have panzerfaust at our disposal, so I want us to start knocking out their armour. If you can kill the crew as well, even better, but our main effort must be reducing their means to fight us. With their armour destroyed, they will be even less keen to fight us in the dark, would you agree?'

Plenty of nods and murmuring from around the room. Dieter continued.

'Dennis and Otto will stay here and man the radio throughout today and tonight, the remainder of us will work on the roadblock, and then at last light we will go down into Schlangen and see what the Americans are up to. Remember guys, don't bite off more than you can chew, we need to ensure we can get away after an attack, understood?'

More nods again, me included. Thomas spoke up.

'Two Faust per man, you will leave one at the roadblock, and take the other into town with you. You never know, we might get some juicy targets. Plus ensure we take enough axes' for the work we need to do, any questions?'

There were none, people started to move about with a purpose, chairs scraped across the wooden floor, time to get ready. Without much direction, the guys formed a human chain on the cellar stairs, as the panzerfausts' and axes' got manhandled up onto the kitchen table. Without waiting to be told, I had slung my MP40 around my body and took the first two Faust on the top of the pile. I then made my way back out into the frost coated garden.

Before long, soldiers began to filter out of the house with all their required gear. Cigarettes were smoked, feet were stamped to try and keep out the cold of the late morning. The breath from everyone was visible in the cold, mixed in with tobacco smoke. In the Senne barrack block, I tried to roll a cigarette from loose tobacco and papers, and made a right cock up of it, much to the amusement of my fellow recruits, the instructor however, who was the intended recipient of my efforts was most pissed off as I dropped his tobacco all over the floor. That cost me a night of polishing the entire barracks' boots. As the last of the men filtered from the kitchen into the gardens, I noticed Gerhard and Felix venturing into one of the many random out buildings that littered the property. Gerhard popped his head out in our direction, and with a low, sharp whistle he beckoned us over to him.

'Here you go boys' he said, pointing to a rusty pile of short, thin metal pickets, just inside the shed door. 'These will do the trick when building up our fighting positions'.

Dieter nodded his approval, 'well spotted, alright guys grab two each, Erik, you can have that hammer over there'.

In the dim interior of the shed, I could just make out the profile of a very sorry looking hammer. It had seen better days, its wooden handle was black, but worn smooth. The head coated all over in rust. The handle was about eight inches long, which allowed me to tuck it down underneath my belt kit. I managed to get away with not having to carry any of the pickets, which suited me, since I had two panzerfaust, and my own weapons to cart up to the roadblock. Once I had readjusted myself and my gear, I was good to go. Gerhard caught my eye line, and gave me a wink and a nod. Let's get on with this.

As one large group we slowly filed out of the gardens, and onto the road that took us back up to the roadblock. The paced was slow and deliberate. We had heavy, cumbersome loads, and yet had to stay alert for the Americans. The attack on the tank crew the other night may have made them exploit further out of Schlangen. They may have discovered the roadblock, and now lay in ambush for us. Who knows? It wasn't long before I was sweating under the weight and the effort of the climb. Looking at the column of guys in front of me, their breath and sweat steam hung over them in the cold air as we moved higher and higher. Just before the crest of the hill we all stopped to have a rest. In typical fashion, coughs and the aroma of tobacco soon filled the air. The only two men who remained standing in the road were Thomas and Dieter; they had shed their marching loads, and were now in just what they wore and their personal weapons.

Dieter spoke, 'you guys wait here, we are going to check out the roadblock for anything out of place'.

With that, both Dieter and Thomas made their way over the summit and out of sight. I turned to Gerhard, who just shook his head and grinned.

'They will have us march to Berlin if they had their way.'

I frowned 'really?'

He nodded once again, 'enjoy the war Erik; history will not be kind to us.'

That sounded familiar, my thoughts drifted to Bobby. He fought like a man who had nothing left to lose, should I fight like that? If I resigned myself to death, would I perform better? Be more reckless? More daring? I sat in silence, listening to the quiet hum of various conversations amongst the group. Before long, Dieter and Thomas returned.

'The roadblock is clear, let's go, we are burning daylight.'

We all clambered to our feet, adjusted ourselves and then trudged on. As we made our way into the roadblock, I was still impressed by our efforts in concealing it. The wind and cold had now made it blend in with the surroundings even more, as if it had always been there. We unloaded all our gear behind the trees crossing the road. Same routine as before, down to just undershirts, but our weapons still on us, less the panzerfausts, which remained stacked with our gear.

Dieter called for order.

'Split into two teams, using the pickets and axes, build up fighting positions on the flanks, facing at an angle into the road in front of these trees. You know what to do; those who don't, listen to the older lads, right get to it.'

We now had two foremen on site for this one, Thomas and Dieter, they remained wrapped up warm and situated with our gear. I stayed with Gerhard, two reasons, I would learn stuff from him, and two, I liked him. Between us, we picked up four pickets and an axe and ventured off to the right flank of the roadblock.

Gerhard took his time siting our fighting position, after a time I had to ask what the problem was. He invited me to take a knee next to him as he pointed back towards the road.

'We need a clear shot at the side of their tanks, I don't want our rockets clipping branches and trees on the way in.' He explained. 'We need to have a strong enough position in order to fend off their infantry who will no doubt be in the woods either side of the road. Plus, our rocket shot will be a one shot deal, their tanks will not allow us a second chance if we miss.'

I now understood. Lessons from Russia no doubt.

We got to work chopping smaller, thinner trees from way back in the woods, so to now give away human interference in the area. The thinner trees made it easier for us to drag them back to our position and then carve and shape accordingly. As we stacked the logs, the pickets staked in either side of the pile helped us stack them reasonably high. Gerhard didn't want them too high, since it would look out of place, no matter how well you concealed it. Once complete, and a sweaty undershirt to prove it, we stood out in front of our position, to see anything that could give away our intentions to the enemy. In the position, the log stack reached about the top of my thigh, which may seem rather high, but out in front next to the road, you really had to take your time trying to locate it. Not bad if I did say so myself. We made our way back to it, and there was one last finishing touch to complete. The mud and leaf litter decorating.

I did have one question for Gerhard. 'What if their infantry are real close when the ambush is sprung?'

Gerhard looked at me with a deadpan expression, 'don't be a hero Erik, throw your grenades, spray a full magazine at them and run!'

Fair enough.

With our position prepared, we made our way back up to where our gear was located. Dieter and Thomas were deep in conversation, not even acknowledging our presence as we got dressed. It was a bright clear day thus far, and bloody cold. There was no mention of us going to help the others, and I sure as hell wasn't going to suggest it. Given the level of experience in the entire group, they knew how to prepare an ambush position, officially I hadn't even finished recruit training yet. Over the course of the next hour or so, the others made their way back to their gear. Once we were all together again, it was mid afternoon and we were starting to lose daylight already. I wondered if I would feel the warmth of a summer on my face ever again. This winter was one of the longest and harshest I had ever known up to that point in my life. We had it pretty easy here. I would guess the weather in the east must have been even worse.

The usual chit chat and tobacco aroma hung over us as the last of those finished with their positions got dressed. Thomas called for quiet.

'Shortly we are going back into Schalngen. We are all going, the aim of tonight's' mission is to knock out as many of their tanks as possible. If there are targets that are too good to miss, we will deal with them too.'

He paused to allow his words to sink in.

'Your Fuhrer demands that you are ruthless with the invader. Give them no quarter; allow them no respite from this war. They are sitting down there like their war is over, but let me assure you of this, theirs is only just beginning.'

I looked around me, the sinister leers on their faces had returned, the sun was going down. I glanced at Gerhard; he remained deadpan, nothing sinister on his face, just professional. Thomas wasn't finished.

'The darkness is ours, comrades. They will fear the darkness.'

Nods all round, and they repeated Thomas.

'They will fear the darkness.'

My stomach tightened with nerves, doubting my own position within this group of men. By day, they were soldiers, with hopes and dreams to talk of. Who laughed and joked at each other's misfortunes. But by night, they became something else, not monsters in the sense, but detached from humanity and decency. They would do whatever it took to win this war, and even if Germany couldn't win it, they sure as hell were going to make the invader pay for it.

What have you got yourself into here Erik?

## 6.

It was as good as dark when we finally set off. If I stood around any longer, I thought I was going to freeze. My feet ached badly in my boots from the cold, my stomach knotted with both hunger and nerves. I wasn't in the mood to drink cold water from my belt kit, I just wanted to get on with what was on the cards tonight, tank hunting. If the other lads were just as cold as me, they never let it show, they were in another place right now, ready to inflict pain and mayhem on the Americans, the sinister grins and glares on their faces gave it all away.

Both Thomas and Dieters teams patrolled out together, I wasn't entirely sure which team I was with for this one, I kept it simple in my head, I would go where Gerhard went. We skirted around the roadblock on the left and made our way down the hill. A fog had settled at the bottom, and as we started moving through it, the night air got even colder. As the tree line on the left started to thin out, we moved into the left ditch. The fog got somewhat thicker as we moved closer to Schlangen. Up ahead the column began to follow the ditch as it crept around to the left. The densely leafed bushes in this portion of the ditch made the front of the column clamber our and skirt around it to the left. It was a pain in the arse to keep doing this, with an MP40 in one hand, and panzerfaust in the other, I would have to find a suitable foothold and climb out with legs only. Some of the guys cursed, as they slipped trying the same method, but we all managed to get out of there, and into the fog laden field. We moved carefully though the fog, the raised bank of the road to our right, and nothingness to our left. There could be a whole battalion of Americans sat out there, and we couldn't see them, nor they us for that matter. Fear began to build up in my mind, and try to take my breath, but I managed to keep it down within me. Just do what the others do. If they are scared, just prey they can hide it too.

The column halted, those up front got down onto their bellies, weapons ready for action. I followed their example. I was on my belly in the cold grass looking left out into the thick fog. Nothing. I could hear whispers from up front getting louder and louder, until Felix in front informed me what had transpired.

'Two vehicles up front, people moving about, fifty metres!'

My stomach turned over. Have we walked right in amongst the Americans? This will be a slaughter if it becomes known. How could we have not noticed this? My mind was racing, building up an image of hundreds of enemy around us looking in, waiting for the order to destroy us all. I hated the fact that I couldn't see them. At least then, you stand half a chance of fighting back. The entire column was on its belly in the middle of a field surrounded by the enemy, what the hell were you thinking? I cursed Thomas and Dieter for this fatal error, with their fancy speeches before a mission, and this is the result. Assholes!

Up ahead, the column began to get to its feet, moving forward again. Are they nuts? Even those behind me were standing up, madness! I looked up at Felix who was gesturing me to follow him. I scrambled to my feet, and moved off after him. The raised bank to our right began to give away other shapes from the fog. Along with a foul, sweet smell, what on earth was that? Out of the gloom was the profile of a tank, on the front of which there were dogs snarling and pulling on a strange shape at the front of the turret. It then hit me what they were eating. Bobby.

The burning bile in me rushed up my throat, by I managed to keep it down. The burning sensation was intense, as I fought not to choke on it. The dogs were eating our dead. What was this world coming to? Why have their bodies not been recovered? Another concept then hit me. Why would the Americans care about our dead? They had their own to deal with I'm sure. As we got closer to the tank, the dogs scampered away off the front into the fog and back into town. I just hoped the dogs wouldn't alert any Americans over there. The group clambered up the broken bank, which may have still contained those buried alive from my former unit, and peered over the top. I made my way up and joined them. The fog the other side of the road was still present, but lighter and we could see through to a certain degree. I strained to see as far as I could down the main road that ran through Schlangen. I couldn't see any movement, with the exception of what appeared to be laundry flapping from almost every window. So people still occupied these houses then? I couldn't see any military vehicles. I could just make out the clucking of chickens, a crying baby, but nothing to suggest anything untoward.

We remained on the raised bank for quite some time, just getting a feel for the situation in Schalngen. The smell on the bank was vile, something was rotting that was for sure, and I knew exactly what it was, but now was not the time to share it. The cold grew more intense. I wasn't the only one feeling it. Even the hardest men in our group were shivering. More whispers generated from my left. Felix kept me in the picture.

'We are crossing the road and going into town from the left side, pass it on'

I passed it on to Gerhard, who merely nodded to acknowledge and in turn informed the guy to his right. It was a few more minutes when the column began to carefully get to its feet. The lads up front walked calmly across the road and down the other bank, making a line for the buildings on the left side of the main road that divided Schlangen. The crossing was without incident, and we all lined up along the side of one of the houses, just tuning into the area before we moved on. The sounds of the night were nothing out of the ordinary. Baby crying, a dog barking, chickens getting excited. The column began to move off to the left, nice and slowly. There was a lot of stop and start, since those up front took care before going around a corner. This continued for some time. We had moved into one particular street, and despite its lack of activity, you couldn't help but notice there was a lot of bed sheets hanging from the windows, white bed sheets. Was it laundry day or something? The column went firm along the wall of one of the first houses, but someone from the front of the column wandered into the middle of the road. Who the hell was that? I then quickly identified the profile belonged to Dieter, the biggest guy in our group. He casually wandered up the middle of the street on his own, as if he was on his way home from work. Last time I saw him do this, he killed a tank crew single handed. The man scared me.

After a short period of time, the lads in the column became restless, and began to question the motives of Dieter to just wander off up the middle of the road. Thomas came down the line to keep order. There was clearly a reason for this rather brash move, but I couldn't think of one at that particular time. I was cold, scared, and our leader had bloody wandered off. Before long, a lone figure appeared from the fog in the middle of the road. The casual stride of Dieter gave him away; he continued down the column and stopped right in front of me. Rather loudly, has asked for everyone to gather around him. This was too weird.

Dieter looked furious. He then stood on tip toe, grabbing the large white bed sheet that was flapping above us, ripping it from its fixtures.

'The good people of Schlangen have appeared to have surrendered, hence the fucking bed sheets from every fucking window. The cowardly vermin.'

Dieter was not happy at all.

'How the fuck are we to continue to fight the invader when our own people give up?' His temper was fraying, and his voice was getting louder. I was starting to get that nervous feeling again.

'We will make an example of someone for this treachery tonight, mark my words. Let's go!'

With that, he stormed off back up to the front of the column, who then fell in behind him and followed. We continued down the street at a steady pace. Not like the cautious moves of earlier. I think we could safely say there were no Americans in this street, at least I hoped there wasn't. We then began to make our way through gardens and out buildings at a more cautious patrol pace. I just hoped Dieters' anger didn't get the better of him, and we ended up in a rather grim situation surrounded by the enemy. We had entered a maze of wire strand fences, chicken huts and out buildings. The column stopped suddenly. I could just make out the sound of music. I thought my mind was playing tricks on me. My suspicion was confirmed when others in the column agreed it was music we could hear. Word came down the line for us to stay put for now, Thomas and Dieter were going for a closer look. We all got down on one knee, facing outwards. Our current position wasn't good for us at all. Nothing but Chicken huts and wire strand fences for cover, over looked by various houses. If these houses were occupied by Americans, it only took one of them to go for a piss in the night out in the garden for it to all go really wrong, really quickly.

It must have only been a couple of minutes, but felt like hours, Thomas and Dieter returned. This time, in a more quiet and controlled manner, they called us forward to gather around them. They looked pleased; this should be the time when I start to worry? Thomas spoke.

'There appears to be a party going on, just through the houses there. There are tanks, but they are covered over, not ready for action. Their crews could well be in these houses.'

He indicated where as he spoke. My stomach turned over. It just takes one to go for a piss. Thomas continued at a whisper.

'It must be some of their brass having the party. There are three jeeps parked outside. Their drivers are looking rather cold and bored, so wont' be ready for us.' He was now grinning menacingly.

'What are we to do?' Gerhard whispered. Dieter jumped in at this point.

'Ignore the tanks; they are not a threat at this point. We will have two groups, mine, including you and Erik will hit the party with the rockets, and Thomas's team will deal with any enemy coming out of the houses. Once we've put the rockets into the house, we will run for our lives straight up the street back towards where we encountered the dogs, clear?'

There were nods all round, seemed straight forward enough. Dieter continued.

'My team, make sure you have a panzerfaust ready for action, we need to hit it quickly for it to have the desired effect. Their other tanks will not race down here in the dark if they hear rocket fire, it will be too risky for them, but their infantry might be upon us real quick, so be on your game.'

The lads dispersed at a crouch, fearful of American troops looking down at them from the houses. I quickly prepared one of my panzershreck for action. I also ensured my MP40 was ready to hand, and my magazines and grenades were in a suitable place for action. I forgot the cold for that moment; I had more pressing issues at hand.

Dieter then led us very slowly down between the houses towards where the music could be heard. The alley way between the houses was very dark, and I took comfort in this. Out in the street there was some commotion coming from a house just out of sight to the left. The entire group all managed to get into the alleyway without much trouble. No one spoke, there was no longer a need for it, and the only sound that was heard was the cold fabric of a rustling smock or the odd scrape of boots on the concrete pathway. We remained in the alley for some time, up ahead I could see Dieter peering around the corner, Thomas leaning out further around him to confirm the target. Thomas then peered off to the right, and in a loud whisper, 'Panzers!' With a snap of fingers, Dieter called his team forward, me included. As we pulled up behind him, he made his way slowly and cautiously across the road. We followed one by one; with all the best will in the world we couldn't silence our boots on the cobbled road. I could see a line of about four tanks parked up, facing north out of town. They were covered up as explained, but their crews could be in any of these very houses, this was getting too much for me to bear.

Once across, we lined up behind Dieter as he carefully led us through the small gardens at the front of a row of houses. We had now entered the garden of the last house in the terrace. The music grew louder as we got closer to the target. Dieter peered around the corner once more, nodding his approval he then briefed us up at a whisper.

'We will line up along this fence', he pointed to the wooden slat fence that led back to the cobbled road. 'There are three jeeps parked outside, and three drivers.' He grinned. I was shitting myself.

'Ignore the drivers; put the rockets through the front door and the large window to the left. You will see it in a minute, the lights are on, and there are people moving about inside. Get into position, don't rush, I don't want the drivers giving us away.'

On my knees and forearms, I slowly made my way down the fence line. I could hear my heart beating loudly in my ears. I was soaked in sweat, despite the short, slow movements we had made. Once in position, I was eye level with the top wooden slat of the fence. With a slight lift, I could see the jeeps easily, the drivers stood in the middle, hands in pockets, every now and again, and their faces would glow with the drag of a cigarette. Dieter crawled down the line, kneeling down just behind me. He put a heavy hand on my shoulder, which almost gave me heart failure.

'Steady lad, you are shaking like a leaf.'

I thought I was okay, but clearly it was evident how much pre match nerves I had.

Across the road to my left, I noticed Thomas' group getting into position in the opposite gardens. They sounded like a herd of elephants in the cold still night, but that must have been me being hyper sensitive prior to combat. Thomas gave the thumbs up. Here we go.

'Get ready', whispered Dieter.

I focused on the large window, with its curtains partially closed. Ignore the drivers Erik, just aim at the window. I saw uniformed figures moving backwards and forwards in the softly lit room. Laughter echoed out into the street, the music appeared to get louder in those final moments.

'Stand up', came another whisper.

My legs burned as I slowly got to my feet, both hands remaining on the panzerfaust. With it on my shoulder ready to fire, I caught the glimpse of a young girl in the window, handing out drinks. I blinked rapidly, there she was again, laughing and smiling as she handed out drinks.

'FIRE!' roared Dieter.

The deafening thud as we all fired our rockets overwhelmed me; I could see her horrified face as the rockets ploughed through the window, the explosions rippling tremendously down the street in the night air. The ringing in my ears muffled out the horrendous weight of fire that smashed the drivers full on. As the ambush subsided, my hearing began to return. Straight away, I was all rather confused. I peered over the fence; I could see Dieter running full sprint at the house, finishing the drivers off with his pistol, shattering their faces in an almost deliberate execution. He then disappeared into the house. What the hell was he doing? The streets around us were now filled with the sounds of crying babies, men shouting, chickens going mad. The spluttering of tank engines coming to life. We really need to be getting out of there, right fucking now.

Dieter came back out into the street, waving us over to him. He even waved over Thomas' group. What the hell was happening? We vaulted the fence and jogged over to him.

'We have prisoners' he announced. I could believe what he just said.

'What fucking prisoners?' Thomas demanded.' We are not here to fuck around Dieter.'

The commotion in the streets around us was getting louder; the Americans could be all over us in a matter of minutes.

'We have a male and a female we can use to our advantage.' Dieter stated, 'we will send a strong message to those who invade us and collaborate with the enemy.'

'What the fuck are you talking about?' Thomas gasped.

Dieter waved him inside, Thomas beckoned me and Gerhard to follow him in. We made our way through into the hallway; the right hand wall was shattered and smouldering from a rocket. The wooden staircase was badly splintered; the narrow strip of carpet running up the centre was smouldering badly. We followed Dieter into the first room on the left, and the entire room was a mess. Shattered furniture and glass. The curtains were smouldering. There were a small number of what appeared to be dead Americans in the room. There was one propped up against the back wall, breathing heavily through a bloodied face, alongside a badly bloodied woman, her dark dress badly torn, she had her hands on her ears. Was this the girl I saw just before we fired? Above us, probably the bedrooms, I could make out the sound of crying children, what a horrible time for them, I felt terrible. What have you done Erik?

# 7.

'Stand up!' Dieter roared at them,' stand the fuck up!'

They both just sat there looking at him, the woman let out a squeal of agony as Dieter dragged her to her feet by the hair. 'Are you deaf you Jewish fucking whore?' He roared in her face.

'She can't fucking hear you!' Thomas shouted at him, 'look at the blood coming from her ears.'

Sure enough, the girl was in a bad way. The soldier on the floor was in no better state. Thomas grabbed him by the shirt, dragging him to his feet, blood was pouring from his ears also. The American was in no condition to resist.

'They come with us', Dieter ordered. He glared at Thomas to get his point across. Thomas glared back, and then with a glancing eye over his American prisoner, shoved him at Gerhard and me.

'Get him outside; he will be coming with us.' Thomas barked.

We firmly hustled our prisoner outside; he was in just a shirt, trousers and boots. The cold air took his breath away. This was the first American I'd ever seen up close. Very much human, not the broad chested movie star I had imagined as a boy. And now he was our prisoner. Outside there was chaos. Foreign male voices could be heard getting closer, vehicle engines, and the squeal of tank tracks rumbling around, dogs going berserk, we had to leave right now. Or we weren't leaving at all.

Thomas and Dieter came out into the street. Dieter still had the girl by the hair. She was groaning and sobbing. She was a real mess. She held Dieters' wrist with both hands, since she wasn't very tall, and Dieter was, to be fair, a colossus of a man in comparison. The blood on her face was beginning to dry and flake, streaks of tears had cut through the blood on her cheeks, making her face look worse than it already was.

'You and your team take him and get back to the roadblock, me and my team have one more thing to do before we leave, go now.' Dieters' order was final.

Thomas merely nodded with a look of contempt for Dieter on his face. He took the American from us, shoving him over towards Johann and Lars. The prisoner stumbled and fell to his knees with a groan. They pulled him roughly to his feet. Thomas took the lead, and led his team off towards the alleyway were we had prepared the ambush, with their battered and bloody prisoner in tow.

Dieter peered down at his quarry,' you my little Jew fucking whore, you are about to serve the Fatherland in a manner befitting your crime.'

She was sobbing too much, her pleas where very loud, she could very well still be deaf from the ambush, hence sobbing loudly. Dieter sneered at her, then flicking his head to us.

'Let's get the fuck out of here!' he barked, best decision he had made all night.

We set off, Gerhard leading, back the way we had entered the town. We had wasted too much time in the ambush area to just run north out of town. Just as we made our way back into the alleyway, with the sobbing girl being dragged along also, there was an almighty thud of grenades in the gardens just beyond, following instantly by heavy chattering gunfire. Had Thomas' group been ambushed? Gerhard waved us to stay put, as he went to investigate. The sobbing girl was getting louder, when I turned to see Dieter grab her by the throat, and talk through gritted teeth.

'Shut your fucking mouth whore!'

Why did he bother? She probably couldn't even hear herself.

Gerhard waved us forward, leading us into the gardens, I followed on quickly. It didn't occur to me that he could lead us into another ambush, I just trusted him, that's all I can really say on that score. As we made our way through the gardens, we encountered two bodies, both American. They were half dressed; face down in the mud, probably one of the tank crews billeted in the house next to us at that point. There appeared to be no casualties from Thomas' group, so we pressed on. The sound of chaos in the streets around us was getting even fucking louder. You'd be forgiven for thinking that with the amount of dogs barking in the area, every bloody household must have owned at least one. What did quickly cross my mind was the fact that they could be American Army dogs, tasked with following our trail. I was just scared at that point; I just wanted to get back to the roadblock as quickly as possible.

Gerhard slowed the patrol pace down once more as we re-entered the street full of white bed sheets swaying slightly in the heavy fog. At this point, I felt a little more confident about our position. The fog slowed everything down for us. We could hear tank engines, and the squealing of tanks tracks on cobbled streets, but their crews would be very wary of panzerfaust teams still lurking in the fog and shadows. Any of their infantry would be moving around with caution, not wanting to get ambushed by us, or one their own patrols. The fog made everything look really spooky at the start of this operation, but now I started to take comfort in it.

My little world instantly shattered when, what sounded like was in the very next street to our left, was a volley of tank and machine gun fire. Tracer flicked skywards, glass smashed, tiles and bricks could be heard collapsing, what the hell was going on over there? I couldn't help but look at Dieter for some inspiration, as he struggled with the girl along the road.

'They are shooting at their own shadows, keep fucking moving boy!'

I wasn't going to argue with the man, I turned and kept my gaze upon the back of Gerhard, who was hopefully leading us to safety. Once clear of the bed sheet street, we carefully picked our way through more gardens, trying not to excite dogs, chickens, and basically anything else that got give away our location to the Americans. At a painfully slow pace and as quiet as possible we crept through the gardens. The only thing that sound horrendously loud was the girls' sobbing, the sound of a sharp slap across her face, followed instantly by a high pitched squeal made me wince. Why were we taking her with us? The thought of her rape suddenly filled me with dread. This girl was German for Christ sake, what the hell are we doing, attacking our own people? This was not right, this world was crazy enough, without this shit getting thrown in too, but what could I do?

We finally made it to the house just before the raised road, where the dogs were eating Bobby's' remains. Gerhard was peering around the corner, back down the main road running through Schlangen. The whole area was slowly quietening down. Dogs still barked, but the sound of enemy armour moving about in the fog had almost gone, and I couldn't hear any voices of enemy infantry nearby. Dieter made his way forward to Gerhard, with the girl still being dragged by her hair.

'Gerhard, I want to leave a little gift for the Americans, and anyone who wishes to collaborate with them.' He emphasised this by pulling the girl fully upright, making her cry out.

Gerhard's' eyes narrowed to a glare. 'Dieter, I am not in the business of punishing our own people. Fighting the enemy yes, but what we are doing right now, is not how it should be done.'

I took this as my cue to side with Gerhard. 'I'm not raping anyone, I don't care who you are. This is wrong Dieter, let her go!'

Dieter looked me up and down with a menacing grin, and a nod of his head.

'I admire your balls boy, I'll give you that, but if you are too squeamish for what is going on around here, then you'd better run back to your mothers' tit.'

I felt anger building up in me, but I knew I was no match for Dieter. It was evident he had killed bigger and better men than me, but there was no need for the girl to be caught up in this. I felt myself welling up slightly.

'Let her go Dieter, she is of no use to us.' Gerhard demanded.

Dieter rolled his eyes, dismissing Gerhard out of hand, using the muzzle of his MP40 to emphasise what he wanted.

'Gerhard, be a good German and take the boy with you over to where the dogs were and wait for me there, is that order too much for you to understand?' By now Dieters' sarcastic facial expression had now become a sinister glare once more. He then pointed his weapon at Konrad and Anton.

'You two come with me, or have you got something to cry about also?'

They slowly shook their heads, their faces giving away a menacing grin. They were loyal to Dieter, which was evident to see.

Gerhard slowly made his way towards the raised bank of the road, his furious glare fixed on Dieter. He then flicked his gaze to me, and with another flick of his head, I followed him. Once up on the road, I turned to see the profiles of Dieter, Konrad, and Anton dragging the girl into the fog. My heart went out to the girl, I dreaded her fate, and I cursed out loud for not helping her more. I could feel my eyes welling up. I looked at Gerhard, who remained his deadpan self. No emotion, just staring into the fog.

'What will happen to her?' I managed whilst fighting the urge to sob.

'He wants to leave the Americans a message, and anyone who cares to interact with the enemy.'

'Will they rape her?' The whole image of it turned my stomach.

'No, Dieter is too angry for that.' This reassured me slightly, but I still dreaded the outcome of this whole episode.

'Did you see how angry Dieter was, when he ripped the bed sheet down?' Gerhard continued, 'Schlangen has capitulated to the enemy. Hence the white sheets hanging from every bloody window.'

'What does that mean?'

Gerhard remained fixed on the foggy street. 'Germany is dying.'

I turned around and looked at the burnt out panzer wedged into the raised bank. The bloated, foul smelling remains of Bobby still slumped over the main gun. The dogs had done a good job on him. They had eaten pretty much most of his face, the skull was clear to see. His black panzer suit was in shreds where they had got access to more edible parts of his body. Gerhard joined me at the front of the tank.

'This was my last position before I found the roadblock.' I said out loud, not taking my eyes off Bobby. 'I knew this man.'

'Where was he from?' Gerhard asked, 'Did he have family?'

'Frankfurt on the Oder, he fought on because he had heard the Russians had overrun the city. He talked of his wife and daughter.'

Gerhard slowly nodded,' dark times my friend, but the sun will shine again very soon, I promise you that, it will shine again, one way or the other.'

I believed him, there couldn't be much left in Germany to continue to resist. What was left to throw at the Americans, the Canadians, the British, and the Russians? The only thing I could think of was Dieter. It sounded ridiculous, but if every town across Germany had one Dieter in it, it's enough to keep this horrible war going on just a little bit longer.

Footsteps behind us snapped me out of my self pity. Dieter, Konrad and Anton appeared from the fog at a jog. As they climbed the bank, steam from exertion lifted from them. Their faces were glazed in a shine of sweat. My stomach turned over. Had they raped her?

'We will stay here till first light, I want to ensure people get the message', Dieter declared.

'What have you done?' Gerhard demanded. Dieter spun on his heels, putting himself nose to nose with Gerhard.

'I have ensured that whoever collaborates with the enemy will endure the same fate, understand?'

Their eyes locked for what felt like forever. I wanted to split them up, but Anton stepped in before me. 'Enough of this, we are meant to be soldiers, get your shit together, both of you.'

They slowly stepped away, still glaring at each other. Dieter broke off first, scrambling down the bank next to the panzer. We all followed him, Gerhard last. We spread out along the shattered bank where my comrades must have still been buried between the halftrack and the panzer. Here we waited for first light. The fog was truly in for the night, the cold became more evident now we were all calming down from the events of the night. My smock offered me little respite from the cold, and there wasn't anything about for me to wrap myself up in. I found myself a semi decent fighting position. I didn't have my digging tool on my belt kit, and that suited me just fine. I didn't want to dig up one of those who fought with me here just the other day. I made myself a comfortable as it was going to be in any case. I placed my MP40, grenades and my remaining panzerfaust on the bank facing upwards. I didn't ready the Faust for action or anything like that, but it was close to hand if needed. I looked either side of me; the other lads had already done the same. That was all we could do for now. Dieter wanted us to stay put till first light. Despite what we had encountered with the girl, I didn't want to be caught out in the open like this when it got light. So far, we had managed to remain undetected due to the fog and darkness. If the fog lifted as it got light, we could very well find ourselves in full view of the Americans. Not good.

My thoughts turned to Thomas and his team. Had they made it back to the roadblock? What of their prisoner? What use was he to us? The Americans were hardly going to leave the area just because one of theirs had been taken. Let's be fair, both sides had come too far just to let something like that disrupt the war. We were losing, that was evident to see, and now merely playing for time. What of these supposed reinforcements from the north? Would they come at all? Maybe they had been sent elsewhere, or destroyed by enemy fighters. Who was to know? Were the Russians in Berlin? How would we know? Would those in command even tell us? If they have Berlin, do we fight on? What does that achieve? More people die, that's all. What happens when the fighting is over? What will come of Germany? Will we become slaves to the conquerors? Is this why we still fight? Keep fighting for the survival of Germany. Or for the survival of the Fuhrer? We learned at school he had done great things for Germany. So how had it now all come to this? Paderborn smouldered on the horizon, enemy troops were in my hometown, and I was dug in on a raised mud road bank waiting for the enemy. What have you got yourself into here, Erik?

My thoughts were interrupted by a loud, echoing scream in the woods behind us. What on earth was that? I look at Gerhard for inspiration; he caught my eye and slowly shook his head. What was going on back there? Movement to my left caught my attention. Dieter crawled up the bank slowly, and peered over the top. The fog was starting to lift, and the early dawn was slowly coming to life. We all followed his action and crawled up the bank. As I peered over the road, the main road was still heavy with fog, but I could make out movement in the road. As the fog and light lifted, I could slowly make out each pair of streetlamps that marked the edge of the cobbled road. I could see humans stood in the road. They were stood beneath a streetlamp, which was not lit. None of them were lit throughout the night. So what was so fascinating about that one? I could now recognise that the humans in the street were both soldiers and civilians. One of the humans was rather taller than the remainder of the group, and very pale. I heard unseen engines splutter into life. The squeal of metal on cobbles. Everyone was gathering around this tall, pale person. There were women in the crowd. I could hear crying. Lots of crying. I then suddenly realise what I was looking at.

Dieter, you fucking bastard!

## 8.

They'd stripped her naked. Fucking naked. Why the fuck would you do that? What was her crime? Just being nice to people. Okay, she was being nice to the Americans, but for fuck sake, she was just being decent. So them bastards stripped her naked, and hung her from a fucking streetlamp like cattle. Why? I could feel myself welling up as I glared at Dieter. He didn't look at me. Anton caught my glare, tears were plain to see running down my cheeks. He didn't smile; he just turned his attention to his weapons before him.

You bastards. Why? What the fuck did that achieve? I blinked rapidly to improve my vision that was impaired by tears. The people were spinning her; I caught a glimpse of something across her breasts. It was a crudely made sign, plain to see.

'American Whore'

This was unreal. As if this whole situation was bad enough. We have now resorted to killing our own, and for what? Will the locals fear us? Will they stop talking to the Americans? All I know is we have now sunk lower than I thought we could go. Deserters, now murderers! I looked over at Gerhard; streaks of tears marked his cheeks. Was she the same age as his daughter? I wasn't sure how old he was. He looked old, that was for sure. War would age a man I suppose. The locals had fetched a ladder; an American soldier was slowly climbing it, perhaps to cut her down. Suddenly, Dieter scrambled up the bank with his last panzerfaust, and stood proudly on the road in plain view.

'What the hell are you doing?' Konrad hissed, rather surprised.

Dieter didn't answer; he put the panzershrek on his right shoulder and operated the firing mechanism. The loud thud of the projectile launching caused my ears to ring; I followed the rocket as it arched towards those trying to cut the girl down. Most had turned to face us, as it skimmed on the road just in front of them and exploded in amongst the soldiers and citizens of Schlangen. I was a loud, dull crump as it exploded. The mass of people literally slumped to the floor as quick as gravity would allow. The light grey cloud that erupted in an instant was mixed with a red mist from their shattered bodies. Their screams and cries hit me instantly. The pale body swung wildly, pieces of her body flicked off her as splinters carved through her. Those in the crowd lay in a crumpled mixed heap of soldiers and citizens. I was stunned to the point where I just couldn't register what Dieter had done. I just looked up at him, lost for words. He directed his menacing glare at me, face full of evil grin.

'This is how we fight this fucking war!'

He then proceeded to drop the launcher and take up his MP40. He remained in the standing
position and started firing single shots down the street. Off to the right, brown and green figures began dashing out from between houses, into the gardens which faced us.

'Infantry!' roared Gerhard.

The remainder of us were up on the bank in a flash. I took aim with my MP40 and began to squeeze off single shots at the green and brown helmets bobbing around in the field. I couldn't tell if I was hitting them, but I wasn't waiting around to see if I had. I scrambled down the bank and skirted right for about five metres then sprinted up the bank again to get back into the fight. Rounds snapped over my head as I got back into position. Gerhard had moved even further to the right, which I thought was madness, since the bank where he veered closer to the enemy infantry in the field. I noticed him throwing a grenade into the field. A loud thud marked by a light grey cloud indicated where he had thrown it. His action appeared to subdue those in the field, but more appeared at the end of the main street.

'Infantry, centre!' roared Dieter, who was still standing defiantly up on the road, rounds snapping
past him, some flicking off the burnt out panzer in a flurry of sparks. Even the gravel near his feet was flicking up due to bullet strikes. Was he mad? I came down the bank once more and sprinted left, moving up into a fighting position just to the left of Konrad, who was taking on infantry on the right side of the street. The girls' body was swinging slightly, flinching as it was hit by rounds from both sides in the fire fight. I quickly got my weapon into the aim, trying to find targets; sweat stung my eyes, my heart pounding in my ears. I managed to focus on the girl, when the blurred green and brown mass behind her became more prominent. Armour.

'Panzer!' I screamed out loud, 'behind the body!'

There was a loud thud just to my left, blasting me in gravel, ears and eyes stinging. That must have been the tank. I sank down the bank, head still swimming, eyes raw. I tried to get the grit from out of my eyes. As my hearing returned, a heavy weight of fire was snapping over where I had just been. Dieters' bellowing made me focus quicker.

'Get up here and fight you little shit!'

I looked up; he wasn't standing so proudly on the road anymore, he had adopted a more life preserving fire position now the American tank had made an appearance. He looked back down at me.

'Yes you, you little shit, your Fuhrer commands it!'

I nodded, now was not the time to argue the merits of our recent action. I got to my knees, and scanned the bank for a position to fight. Konrad and Anton were working as a pair, each one moving whilst the other was firing. Fighting for their lives.

'Gerhard!' roared Dieter over the horrendous din of bullet snaps that came through, just above his head. 'The Panzer has gone right, get ready!'

Gerhard came dashing down the line towards us, grabbing both Anton's' and Konrads' panzerfaust from their original positions.

'Erik, with me, lets' go!' Gerhard commanded.

He scrambled away, with me hard on his heels. We moved along the base of the bank as quickly as we could. There was no snapping over our heads this far right. The Americans kept their fire on the centre of the position. I stayed at the bottom of the bank as Gerhard crawled up, peering over the top. With the slow shake of his head, I could tell it was bad news.

'We are going to have to cross the road. We are too far to ensure a first round hit.'

My heart sank; this bank was all that separated us from the enemy, who had tanks, and lots of infantry.

'Let's go!' he snapped as he took off, out of sight. I scrambled after him, praying that the Americans didn't see our daring move across. The ditch on the other side was full of brambles, which caused me to wince as I fell into them face first. Gerhard was in no better position, but grinned at me nonetheless. We very quickly untangled ourselves from or thorny shackles and continued on our hands and knees along a drainage ditch of sorts that ran almost parallel with the farthest right of the gardens, and out houses. I could hear the Americans shouting at each other over the din of a grumbling, rattling beast. I couldn't see it yet, but the ditch we were in was vibrating more and more. Gerhard grabbed my arm.

'Get that thing ready!' he whispered, indicating my panzerfaust. 'Keep low; do not let their infantry see you.'

I didn't need reminding of that fact, I just nodded, carefully getting the panzerfaust ready to fire whilst laying on my front in the muddy, wet ditch. It was awkward, but I managed it. I then, with my arms carefully raised my profile so I could peer over the lip. The tank rattled into view, it was trying to carefully creep around the side of the house, but was chewing up the wire strand fences as it crushed its way through the gardens. Its entire body was draped in sandbags and short lengths of spare track. Up on the turret one of its green and muddy crewmen was manning their huge machine gun. I was certain that if he turned, he would see us lying there, but he appeared more occupied with Dieter and the other two in the centre. Gerhard gave me a nudge.

'Let it pass, shoot it up the arse!' he whispered.

Not what I wanted to hear, but made sense, there was too much crap draped all over the thing to knock it out. It fired its main gun, my ears burst into a high pitched scream, my head instantly thick and swimming. A huge geyser of gravel and road bank instantly showered over the middle of Dieters' position. With a bit of luck, the Americans had killed the bastard. This tank commander was feeling rather confident. No infantry had followed him around the house, why would they? They had us pinned in the middle. To their credit, Konrad and Anton were making it look like there were more of us than there actually were, with their constant changing of fire positions. The tank rumble and screeched further forward towards the road. Its back side was slowly presenting itself to us; the angle was slowly becoming more in our favour. The crewman up on top was really giving it some with the machine gun. Its dull bass drum beat hammered Dieters' position almost constantly. It was the only time I wanted an American to be accurate.

'Get ready!' Gerhard ordered, just above a whisper.

My stomach turned over as I got up into a semi squatting position. The tank was creeping further away, its back end now fully exposed to us.

'NOW!' Gerhard gasped.

The loud thud of the launcher rendered me deaf once again. There was a huge burst of sparks dead centre on the backside of the tank. The impact knocked the gunner up top off his aim and was sprawled over his machine gun. Heavy black smoke began pouring out of the back decks almost instantly, the engine coughing and spluttering out of action. The lumbering beast rolled to a stop. Gerhard grabbed my arm.

'Lets' go!' he shouted.

I ditched the launcher, and sprinted after him back the way we had come. Straight into the mire of brambles that pierced and scratched at our skin and uniforms. Behind me, the squeak and heavy clatter of turret hatches could be heard. I glanced back, its crew, some smouldering were scrabbling out of their stricken vehicle. They were more concerned with rolling around on the grass, putting out their smouldering clothing, than dealing with us. We got free of the brambles when our entire world became the focus of the enemy's' fury. Mud, grass and gravel flicked up all around us, the horrendous din of snaps and whizzes dominated our immediate area. On our hands and knees, we scrambled like maniacs across the road back to the relative safety of the other side.

Soaked with sweat, breathing like it was my last, we both laid at the base of the safe bank, catching our breath. That was fucking close.

'We can't stay here, let's move!' Gerhard ordered, as he clambered to his feet. He set off at a crouch back towards the centre of our original position. I stumbled to my feet and followed. When we got back to the centre, I was disappointed. Dieter was still alive. He was wounded, a large long gash along the side of his face was evident, the blood very fresh. The other two were no longer dashing about like maniacs'; they were checking their magazines at the base of the bank. The snaps coming over the top were constant now, with shots flicking up the gravel and mud on the top every so often. Dieter grinned at me offering his hand.

'Good kill there boy, nice shooting!'

I just looked at his hand and then stared back at him. I was in no mood to be associated with this arsehole. His devilish grin now gone. He glanced at Gerhard, who had nothing more than a glare for him too. Dieter nodded, almost as a sign of capitulation.

'Are we ready to go?' he called out.

'Ready!' Anton and Konrad barked out loud. Dieter nodded once more.

'Get your grenades ready, on my order we throw them straight down the street, clear?'

We all understood, lets' just get the fuck out of here.

Grenades at the ready, Dieter crawled to the top of the bank, hold out his right arm at shoulder level. 'Get ready'

We all creeped up the bank, just short of the lip in which the odd round was still flicking up debris.

'NOW!' Dieter roared.

I threw that grenade as hard as I could, to the point where I thought I had injured myself in doing so. Three grenades arched almost effortlessly towards the mass of enemy and civilian dead and wounded in the street. Those who came to their aid scrambled out of the way to avoid our grenades. They bounced and settle amongst those already dead at the base of the hanging girl, who was now nothing more than a pale and bloody carcass you would see in a butcher's window. As they exploded, shreds of bone, muscle and clothing flicked all over the street. The girl slammed face first into the bloody, cobbled street, her noose finally cut by grenade splinters. There was an instant loud thud just to our right, which stunned me, causing my right side to throb and my ear to ring. Who was shooting at us?

'FOLLOW ME!' roared Dieter as he took off over the road, towards the enemy dead and dying.

Before I could even comprehend what he had just done, Anton and Konrad were up and over, firing as they went, roaring at the top of their voices. This was just madness. I looked to see if Gerhard was following, he wasn't there, why? Gerhard, why? Of all the people, why would you entertain this madness anymore?

'Down here boy.'

I spun around; at the bottom of the bank was Gerhard, a bloody hand clasping his chest, his weapon still in the other. He had blood around his mouth and running from his nostrils. I slid down the bank to tend to my old friend.

'I got hit as I threw the grenade' he managed between blood spraying coughs, 'I only just managed to get it over the road.'

Hence the explosion next to me.

I was welling up as I tried to pull his hand away to inspect his wound. He kept it firmly in place. Despite being gravely wounded, he was still strong as an ox.

'Leave it boy, its okay.' He murmured through blood smeared lips.

Over the road, all hell had broken loose, the weight of fire was horrendous, the Americans were now giving those three their undivided attention. Why would they do such a thing? Haven't enough people died today? I felt Gerhard's' hand on my elbow.

'You must go now Erik, get back to the roadblock, you don't have to be here anymore.'

I wiped my tears with my torn, muddy sleeve. 'What about you?'

'I've had my war Erik, you need to go and have yours, please' he coughed up more blood,' go boy, the Americans will not spare you, please go now.'

The weight of fire was petering away over the other side; they would take this position anytime now.

'Go Erik, get away from here, you are just a boy, don't waste it by looking after an old fool like me.'

He shoved his weapon at me and gave me a clip around the ear, 'go now!' he barked.

I'd passed the point where I could hide my sobbing and got to my feet. He looked such a sorry broken mess laying there; he just nodded at me, and waved me away. I was beside myself, having to abandon a friend to the enemy. I turned and began to run along the base of the bank once more, this position had once more destroyed any friendships I had forged in that awful fucking mess. What have you got yourself into here Erik?

## 9.

I'd made it into the roadside ditch some way up towards the roadblock, when I paused for breath. I slumped on my back wiping the tear streaks from my face. I truly was in a world of shit. I just wished it would all be over soon. I didn't have a clue how I was going to make it home. If I surrendered, the Americans would probably shoot me out of hand, or even worse, hand me over to the Russians. Maxs' threat still remained with me. No one was taking SS prisoners, no one. We were going to pay dearly for this war that was for sure.

Through the trees I could still just make out the knocked out Panzer and Halftrack, and the banked road. I could see lots of human movement on the road between the two vehicles. Americans. The roar of their tank engines echoed loudly in the woods I was sat in. An armoured vehicle of some sort crept into view to the left of the position, more troops jumping off the back of it. Thick black smoke marked the far right of the enemy positions, the tank I had knocked out. I caught a glimpse of flame as it licked the scorched shell of the vehicle. There would be a loud pop now and then as what may have been its ammunition cooking off, sparks would erupted and shower the field it was sat in. Behind the burning furnace that was the tank, I could just make out the shimmering profile of soldiers and what looked like more armour. The vehicle on the left edge of the position fired its main gun into the wood line directly behind our original position. It made me jump. The echo was horrendous. It followed up with a long burst of machine gun fire, red tracer punched deep into the wood line, the odd tracer would flick off in random directions. A loud series of snaps had me on my belly in the ditch. The tanks behind the burning wreck fired into the wood line I was sat in. Their tank rounds thundered passed behind me, deep into the dark woods. Followed immediately by a hornets' nest of tracer, snapping all over the place. Gravel and mud, flicked up here and there in front of me. They were taking no chances. Searching fire, in case there were more of us. I could make out the loud roar of horsepower as those on the right pulled up onto the road. They were pushing forward. My stomach turned. I could not stay here. With that I was scrambling along the bottom of the ditch, trying to make some distance between the Americans and myself. Before long, I was just coated in mouldy leaf litter and mud, trying to keep as low as possible, and make good speed. More tank rounds thundered through above me. Almighty echoes of explosions, and the loud sharp crack, as trees got smashed, crashing to earth, dragging canopy with it. One tree received a direct hit not far from the ditch I was in. Pale timber splinters of various sizes, showered me, adding to the mire I was already coated in. If I had to fight all of a sudden, my weapon would have failed; it was coated in all sorts of shit. Max would have kicked my arse on the Senne for such a crime.

The firing became the odd thunder of tank shell and the odd ripple of machine gun fire. Maybe turning the Teutoburg Wald into match wood was taking up too much of their ammunition, but that suited me fine. What weren't going away were the constant throb of tank engines, and the metallic squeal of tracks on cobbles. Were they slowly following me down the road? Humouring me, waiting for me to just get tired and give up. I dared not look back, and just kept scrambling forward. Just short of a prominent bend in both the ditch and the road, I had to stop. My hands were just a mass of splinters, cuts, and caked in mud. I was steaming in the cold air due to my efforts. My heavy breathing was very prominent too. I just hoped their gunners were more interested in breakfast, than peering through their sights looking at a very sweaty, and steaming German soldier in a ditch. They had stopped, which was a relief, I could clearly make out two tanks, side by side. Both turret crews were talking to each other. Two poured over a map, and the other two were lighting each others' cigarettes. In the shimmer of their exhaust fumes, I could make out their infantry crossing the road from left to right, moving into the forest that led the way up to where I was currently slumped. They were planning to come up this road; I couldn't enjoy the view anymore. I needed to warn Thomas and the other guys.

I remained in the ditch for as long as I could, once I was confident I was out of line of sight from the enemy, I clambered onto the road and broke into a jog. No time could be wasted getting back to the roadblock. I looked a sorry state to whoever happened to see me at this point, but I didn't give a shit. As I began the ascent up to the false horizon, I couldn't even see the road block, that's how much effort we had put into its construction. With a bit of luck their turret crews wouldn't see it till the last possible moment. I moved back into the ditch, and as I climbed higher, I could just start to make out some of the tree branches of those lying across the road. I began to carefully pick my way around, nothing that I hadn't done before, when I notice a groaning and what could only be described as sobbing. I stood still, trying to focus on where it was coming from. Animal? Possibly livestock? Apart from the strange groaning, I could only hear the branches above us in the canopy creaking and swaying. I then heard what may have been a cough, followed by a loud groan. It was coming from above me, on the logs. I made my way back around to the front and carefully climbed up.

Oh my fucking God!

I felt what remained of any food in my stomach fight its way up into my mouth. In a vain hope to hold it down, it burnt my nostrils' as it found another way out. I collapsed to my hands and knees' on the first log, wretched my life away in stomach ripping spasms. Once I managed to get it under control, I cuffed away the string like vomit from my lips, and had to look again.

The American.

Naked as the day he was born. Dried blood all over his face and chest. Both ears now just a clotted mass of blood and leaf litter. Ankles pinned to the second log with one of the metal pickets. Smashed clearly with some force through his ankles. Fresh blood slowly coated blood already clotting underneath. His feet and ankles bloated black and purple, looking fit to burst. His hands looked no better, palms uppermost, purple, black and swollen, a picket hammered through each one.
He groaned, gargled, spluttering fresh blood over his own face, and occasionally sobbed. I picked myself up and stood over him. I carefully made my way around the left side of him, he yelped in a gargling splutter as I stood on the log his legs where staked to. I apologised under my breath for the discomfort, gingerly placing my feet where I felt I wouldn't cause him any more suffering. I avoided the log his hands where skewered to. He appeared to struggle to hold his head still. I squatted down to investigate, his sudden outburst caused me to jolt and almost fall of the blood roadblock altogether.

'Nooooo' he gargled, 'gren-ade, gren-ade!'

'Don't touch him!' came a voice above me.

I snapped left, seeing Thomas stood on the farthest log. He held his MP40 in both hands, his face a sneering, menacing leer, full of wickedness, void of any compassion.

'Gren-ade?' I enquired.

The leer became a grin, 'look under his head.'

I put my left cheek to the log and peered underneath the Americans' head. His head was perched on what I assumed was a grenade of some description; I couldn't confirm its design, since it was caked in dry blood, and the soldiers' hair.

'Took them from those bastards who ambushed us in the gardens. You must have heard it.'

I did recall the aftermath of a vicious exchange as we made our way out of Schlangen. Two dead enemies face down in the gardens, minus their grenades clearly. I nodded my acknowledgment. I was too tired and afraid to question anyone on the events of last night and this morning. I wasn't quite sure who I feared more now. The Americans or my own side. We had clearly entered the realms of the surreal. Desperate, spiteful measures by desperate, spiteful men.

'Where are Dieter and the others?' Thomas enquired.

'He hung the girl for the Americans and locals to find her.' I paused to see if there was so much as a glimmer of humanity left in the man.

Nothing. He remained in his demonic state. 'And?'

'Dieter ambushed the group trying to cut her down. He killed both the enemy and the locals who came to help.'

The menacing leer returned,' go on!'

I continued, 'we got into a fight with infantry and armour. Gerhard and I knocked out one panzer, and some infantry, but there was just too much to keep at bay. We threw grenades, Dieter, Anton and Konrad charged the enemy. I remained with Gerhard who was badly wounded.'

There was a flicker of human in his expression, 'is Gerhard dead?'

'I don't know, he told me to get back here and warn you.'

'Warn us?' the leer returned. 'About what?'

'They have panzers and infantry moving up towards here.'

Thomas' whole demeanour changed instantly, less demonic, more professional,' show me!'

We scrambled down the logs, the American continued to gargle and sob as we left him. I led Thomas into the woods just off to the right side.

'Just as the road goes out of sight, there are at least two panzers, and infantry in the woods on this side. I don't know about the other side though.'

Thomas scanned where I was pointing with his binoculars, and then nodded his approval of my information.

'Good boy, come with me.'

We made our way behind the roadblock, and there were the remainder of the guys. Including Dennis and Otto. Both armed with MG42, and draped in belt ammunition, ready to fight. He got them into a huddle.

'The boy has just returned from Schlangen. Dieter killed the girl, and the rest of his team trying to be a fucking hero.'

As he paused, I noticed some of the guys glancing at each other, slowly shaking their heads. Could they have some compassion towards the poor girl, or the guys we had lost, who knew?

'Erik informs me that the Americans are moving up here with panzers and infantry. At this time we know there is infantry in the woods on the right, with at least two panzers on the road.' He paused and pointed at Lars.

'Move forward on the left, and try and see if there are any infantry on your side, then get back to me quickly, so I can site you all effectively.'

Lars nodded, stood up and pushed around to the left of the roadblock. Thomas turned his attention to the remainder of us.

'We have limited recourses; we must hit them hard and then withdraw. If we can break clean from the ambush, we will fall back to the house. If we become separated, and the enemy are on your tail, stay away from the house, do you understand?'

We all nodded. I started to shiver and sweat with pre battle nerves again. Do you ever lose them? Or is it because you know what's going to happen?

Our concentration on the up and coming ambush was interrupted by a dreadful, gargling cough from our prisoner, crucified on the logs.

'What about him?' Viktor enquired.

'He stays there; the lead tank will have a nice surprise.' Thomas grinned. Felix chuckled into his sleeve, face full of wickedness. I felt a nudge; I looked up, Johann grinning at me.

'You okay?'

I just nodded, when would this all end?

I could hear heavy laboured breathing when Lars dashed back behind the logs with us. There was a slight pause as get got his breath back.

'No infantry on the left, two panzers up front, staggered. Infantry on the right.' He gasped.

Thomas spun on us immediately.

'Panzerfaust on the left, MGs' on the right. We hit the panzers first. Machine gunners, kill as many infantry as you can, but your main job is to prevent them from getting over the road, understood?

We all nodded, the group then scattered to their various positions. I was at a loose end, when Thomas laid eyes on me once more.

'Erik, go with Otto, help him with his MG42.'

I nodded, and made my way carefully over to the right, trying to find our positions we had prepared the day before. I heard the click of fingers, and noticed Otto waving me over. Just short of his position, I got down on my belly and crawled Into the position. I didn't want any steely eyed enemy noting where I had taken cover and give our position away.

'Right boy, stay on my left side, and help with the ammunition.' Otto commanded. I ensured the belt ammunition was the right way around and ready to feed into the gun. Otto adjusted the sights for the conditions we would be fighting in. Minimum range, close fighting. He also placed his stick grenades just in front of me.

'When I say so, throw one just out to our front. I don't want their infantry coming in on top of us, okay!'

I couldn't agree more. That would be very bad. Our side of the ambush was simple. We didn't open fire until the rockets hit the tanks. With them taken care of, we stand a better chance of taking care of the infantry. All in all, we had about a thousand rounds for our gun, probably the same for Dennis' so short, controlled bursts were required to make it last. The throbbing of tank engines began to echo through the roadblock. Now it was just a waiting game. The thing that would test our nerve was staying quite until the tanks were at the logs. This could well mean that their infantry could already have passed through, should they happen to be leading. Hitting the tanks with their infantry behind us was not something I looked forward to. I'm not a tactician, but I would have my infantry forward in order to detect or spring any tank trap. The engine noise grew louder. I could now hear the squeal of tracks. I peered around the left of our cover, logs built up with the metal stakes. I forgot to check if the leaf litter still coated the outside. On my stomach I could see very little. I didn't want to kneel up, and give us away, so I had to make do. The road rose up and to my left, the branches and splintered ends of the road logs were visible from our side, but coated in mud and leaf litter on the opposite. From ground level, I could just make out the light grey plumes of tank exhaust, which told me that they we about to start the climb up to the logs. The overgrown ferns prevented me from seeing any infantry; they could be right in front of us for all I knew. Otto gave me a gentle nudge on my right shoulder.

'Two panzers, thirty plus infantry.' He mouthed.

I felt nauseous. Two MG42 against a platoon. If we knock out the tanks, we stand a fighting chance.

The change in engine pitch indicated they had begun the climb up to the roadblock. My hands were sweaty, my heart pounding in my ears. Something that seemed to happen to me just before all hell would be let loose. I peered down at my MP40. It was still coated in all sorts of crap. I cursed myself for not taking the opportunity to at least check that it would work. You fool Erik!

'The infantry is leading.' Otto updated me. I knew the Americans would, I don't know why I was so surprised. If anyone was going to fuck up your plan, it would be the enemy.

Otto nodded at the grenades, 'get ready!' he mouthed.

I took hold of one of them, my hands visibly shaking. I tried to prepare it, but I was losing the battle with the shakes. Otto gently placed his left hand on mine, and gave me a wink. It had the desired effect. He slowly drew his hand away, and I was no longer shaking, he knew I was scared, and now was not the time to mock me. He needed me ready to fight, so his fatherly gesture went a long way. I was ready, all I needed to do was arm it and throw.

The roar of the engines as they made their climb sounded terrifying. They couldn't have seen the crucified American yet, yet his screams and shouts were getting more hysterical. When the thunderous engine noise almost became too much, I peered around our cover, and saw the muddy green cluttered profile of the tank turret climb high and left. It must be at the logs by now. The ends of the logs nearest us rocked. The Americans' scream went right through me. The tank had hit the logs. The engine gave out an almighty roar, as the turret lifted, climbing the first log. Its turret crew were down in their fighting positions, not exposed, maybe their periscopes wouldn't allow them to see the obstacle. I could hear foreign voices just the other side of our position shouting and hollering, at who I didn't know, but they then began to whistle and allsorts, maybe to get the tanks' attention.

A dull thud, echoed over the engine noise, as the American was detonated all over the front of the lead tank. His struggle with the grenade was at an end. Red strands of body tissue, wood bark and timber splinters coated the tank. In an instant, the tank was overwhelmed by bright showers of sparks as the rockets found their mark. Their detonation dulled as they penetrated steel. Otto's' MG42 burst into life in short, sharp rippling bursts. Without even looking at me, he barked orders.

'Throw the fucking grenade!'

I knelt up and before us was their infantry, in spades. All were running about, the odd muzzle flash gave away their positions. Some were cut down by Dennis' MG off to our right. I threw the grenade into what I felt was a cluster of enemy troops and got back into cover. I didn't even wait around to spot where it landed. I could just make out the dull thud as it went off over the deafening chatter of Otto's' bursts. The odd snap of incoming passed overhead, along with the splintering crunch as their rounds hit our cover. The outrageous roar of engine and transmission could be heard, but from where I was I couldn't see the vehicle in question. Otto continued with his short and sharp bursts. I made myself useful and made sure there was enough slack in the ammunition belt so he didn't get a stoppage. I noticed movement up on the roadblock. The tank was now just a column of pitch black smoke, its crew trying to abandon their stricken vehicle. Some of them bundled out over the side, down our side of the bank. Dennis had the angle to take care of them. His bursts shattered the crew as they attempted to escape. They were easy pickings, slumped in a dull green pile in a muddy wet ditch. Less troops to fight.

The incoming fire from the infantry was sporadic at best. Our careful preparation of our positions clearly paid off. They began to give up ground, leaving their wounded where they fell. Some made the heroic attempt to recover their comrades, but were ruthlessly cut down but our MGs'. The loud, bass drum beat of a heavy machine gun entered the fray. I couldn't see where it was. It may well have been the other tank engaging the rocket teams, I had no idea. Otto roared out at the top of his voice, scaring the shit out of me.

'Panzer in the woods!'

I carefully peered over our cover; the second tank was pushing into the wood to support its infantry. It was held at bay by the large tree stumps and fallen trees we had arranged. The heavy machine gun on top had a good angle on Dennis' position, as it slowly disintegrated his cover with heavy bursts. Dennis and Johann were no longer fighting, but merely cowering from the enemy firepower now concentrated on them. Otto fired bursts in order to deal with the troublesome gunner, but he just couldn't get the angle.

'Get them rocket arseholes over here, or were are fucked!' He roared.

As I turned to make the suicide dash around the roadblock, Felix must have heard Otto's' request, since he was crawling like a mad man, with two panzerfaust across his forearms. I waved him into our cover. He was gasping for breath, sweating like a beast.

'We killed the first panzer, damaged the one in front of us!' he gasped.

Otto didn't even look at him, 'Well go kill the fucker, or we are in trouble!'

I looked at Felix, who merely rolled his eyes, and prepared one of the rockets. He handed me his MP40.

'Come with me, I'm going to need protection.'

He couldn't be serious. But I dare not refuse. I checked to ensure there was a round in the chamber ready to fight. Once done, I gave him the nod.

Felix flipped onto his stomach and crawled off to the left, straight into the roadside ditch. I crawl like a maniac straight in after him. So far, so good. It was about thirty metres before we would be in a suitable firing position, and we needed to be quick, Dennis and Johann were in trouble. Their cover was now nothing more than splintered timber. Felix took off at a fast pace. He was breathing so heavily, I was scared it would give us away. We had to literally clamber over the shot up tank crew in order to stay in cover. My stomach turned over, they were still warm. Still bleeding out. One of them was groaning. Otto's' consistently short bursts reassured me that we had covering fire, but it felt like the longest thirty metres of my life. We got to where we needed to be. The tank was nose in to the woods just to the right of our ditch. Its right side was already badly scored and chipped; the equipment hanging on the side was smouldering from the initial ambush. The gunner up on the turret was too engrossed with destroying Dennis and Johann to notice us. I push myself as far right in the ditch as possible, so I didn't get my head taken off with the back blast from the launcher. Felix sprung up into the kneeling position and fired. The loud thud of the launched projectile once again turned the soundtrack of battle into just one long, constant ring in my ears. I felt the thud of impact as it hit the tank, slap bang in the side. A huge flurry of sparks showered the immediate area. I was already on my belly, crawling like a man possessed back down the ditch, since I already had the experience of the enemies fury towards anti tank teams.

Once I had made it past the dead tank crew again, I was back level with mine and Otto's' position before I looked back. My heart sank. Felix was still in the position where he fired the rocket, minus his head. Even from where I was, I could see he was still in the kneeling position, slumped against the left side of the ditch. His blood turned his filthy tunic black. The smoking launch tube lay across his thigh. He had done his job however. The tank was smouldering pitch black smoke from its engine decks. As my hearing improved, I heard the rippling bursts from both Dennis and Otto's' MGs' as they destroyed the tank crew as it bailed out. No quarter given.

The infantry had lost the stomach to continue. They slowly moved back, firing as they went. It wasn't landing anywhere near us, the odd snap above us splintered the canopy. Before long, there was no more gunfire. All I could hear was the crackling, popping and fizzing of two burning tanks, one of which still had an engine running. Immediately to our front I began to pick up the groaning of their wounded.

'Friendlies coming in!' came a voice behind us, as Thomas led Lars and Viktor into our position.

They kept their weapons close at hand as they slumped just behind us. Dennis and Johann came in from their position, carrying their smouldering MG by the carrying handle, almost out of ammunition. They look rather worse for wear, but that could be understood, given the circumstances. Some coughed and spluttered, whilst others rolled cigarettes. Apart from groaning wounded, and the crackling, popping of burning tanks, all was rather tranquil again.

## 10.

There was no chat whilst we rested. The adrenalin of the whole situation had gone, for the time being. The aroma of tobacco gave me a lovely feeling of warmth. I was almost in envy of those who smoked, by choice alone I had denied myself one of the last pastimes that you could call your own. Smoking. Such a simple pleasure during dark times such as now.

'We need to finish here, and get back to the house.' Thomas stated, 'I don't think we will see the Americans any more today.'

There were nods amongst the group; the smokers enjoyed the last drags on their cigarettes. We slowly got to our feet, and got our gear together. Our loads would be considerably lighter going back to the house, since we had used almost all of our belt ammunition. We had but a couple of panzerfaust left with us. There were more at the house. I never thought to ask how they managed to obtain such a vast amount of ammunition and weaponry; I think at this stage of the war, scrounging was the name of the game for the German Army. I collected up the grenades from our position, stuffing them into my belt. My sorry looking MP40 that had to be cleaned immediately once back at the house. Otto took care of the MG42, and the small amount of belt ammunition.

Just as Lars began to lead off, Thomas put his hand on my shoulder.

'There is one more thing we need to do. I need your help.'

I nodded, as I peered around at the remainder of the group, the evil grins had returned. My stomach tightened. Was I in trouble?

'Have I done something wrong?' I quietly asked.

Thomas shook his head with a smile, 'good God no Erik, you have fought bravely today, we just need to sort out Felix, that is all. Not an easy task, but it must be done.'

I nodded. Fair enough. Not ideal, but there it is.

Lars then took his leave and led the way for the others, whilst I followed Thomas back over towards Felix. You got used to fighting from a particular position, but when you actually go forward, you see it from a totally different perspective. Their infantry had plenty of cover in which to exploit, even to a point where they could outflank us in the woods. Maybe the Americans really did fear the forests. We came to be stood next what was left of Felix. His top half was black with his blood. I could just make out the top of his spine. Half of his face was lying on his shoulder like and empty rubber mask. My stomach churned. The remainder of his torso was shredded from gunfire. The wall of the ditch kept him propped up, which in turn invited more enemy fire. Truly grim. Anything of value probably couldn't be recovered from his shattered body.

The immediate area was littered with enemy dead and wounded. For the dead, it was over for them. As for the wounded, it meant a long, slow, cold night in a German forest. Thomas walked slowly amongst the dead and dying. The groans and fidgeting of the wounded gave them away. One of whom attempted to get onto his hands and knees. Thomas stood next to him as he slowly got himself up. Thomas made his way slowly until he was facing the head of the wounded American, who had to muster all his strength just to look up at the German. The soldier mumbled something under his breath, which I couldn't understand. Thomas glared at the American, slowly drawing his pistol from its holster. My stomach flipped immediately. The true nature of my task became apparent. Thomas pointed the Luger at the Americans' face. His own face full of hate.

'Heil Hitler!'

The Americans face collapsed with the sheer energy of the bullet, which blew out the back of his skull. The shattered head, still attached at the neck thudded straight back to the ground. The body remained in the kneeling position, with its backside in the air. The whole act made me wince, but it didn't shock me. We had new rules, which was plain to see. I was determined not to fall foul of them rules. I wanted to live. I was certainly more scared of my own countrymen than the enemy. I just stared at the body, empty of emotion.

I caught Thomas' gaze. 'Erik, show no mercy.'

He offered me the pistol grip of his Luger. I was shocked by his order. I was to be his executioner. If I refused, it could well be me lying next to the enemy. I took it from him, this pistol grip still warm. My use of pistols was minimal at best. We didn't really get into pistol shooting on the Senne. We had basic instruction, not much else, more of a weapon for panzer crews and Officers. After Thomas' initial shot, I knew there was a fresh round in the breach. I looked around my immediate area for my first victim. A blood curdling cough gave one of them away, I slowly made my way over. He was laying face down, his torso moving as he breathed heavily. I took the time to think how I was to turn the man over. What if he grabbed me? I looked up at Thomas, who just glared at me, almost daring me to refuse. The soldier still had is helmet on. If I was to just put the muzzle under the rim that would do the job. I bent over, my shaking hand causing the barrel to rattle against the helmets' rim. I could hear him sobbing; he knew it was his time. Executed by a child of all things. I looked up at Thomas, whose' arms were crossed, face full of a wicked leer, nodded his approval. I pulled the trigger.

His head shattered as instantly as the pistol snapped back in my hand. I stood up, my boots were speckled with the man's' blood. Thomas walked towards me, hand outstretched. I handed back the pistol. He patted me on the shoulder.

'Go behind the roadblock, wait for me there.'

I nodded. Numb could be the best way to describe how I felt at that time. I'm pretty certain I had taken lives, but to kill someone up close was a whole new experience. I made my way up to the back of the logs. I flinched every time I heard Thomas finish off another wounded American. The pistol shots echoed loudly through the trees. Thomas was taking his time, clearly enjoying his work. Before long, there were no more shots. He appeared where I was waiting.

'Let's get out of here; I'm hungry and ready for coffee.'

Food was the furthest thing from my mind at that precise moment, despite the fact that my last meal was before we went up to finish off the fighting positions. We trudged down the road, back towards Berlebeck. I couldn't think of anything to talk about. All my energy was starting to drain from me. The ambush at the house In Schlangen felt like a lifetime ago. The girl. Her image came to the front of my mind. Why did we have to kill the girl? Killing the enemy, wounded or otherwise was something I could stomach better than murdering a girl who was just trying to be hospitable in such a shit situation. Were we at a time where we could literally get away with murder? Did the war throw all of societies' rules out the window? What have you got yourself into here Erik?

Johann greeted us as we neared the house. All the blackout curtains were in place, despite it just starting to turn dusk. The days were still short, and cold. Thomas ordered him to stand watch from inside the house. The idea being, that if enemy infantry scouts spot a lone sentry, it usually means he is guarding a position. I was tasked with helping him arrange one of the rooms upstairs to be made into a watch tower of sorts. With no light in the room, we only hung one sheet of blackout material in the window frame, so you could peer through it. If there were enemy in the town, it would be easier to creep into the basement and warn everyone for action. Once complete, word came around for everyone, less Johann who was on watch to gather in the kitchen. As I entered the kitchen, coffee was doing the rounds. Viktor had some potato and vegetable mix going on in the large pot on the stove. The conversation was rather subdued compared to our previous meetings. Partially due to maybe what had transpired over the last twenty four hours, but mainly due to our lack of numbers. Everyone had a seat at the table. Thomas at the end. Large chunks of bread, almost stiff with staleness were in everyone's hands. No one was really fussy at this point, just hungry.

Everyone ate their bread in silence. I was tired, everyone was tired. The only person still on their feet was Viktor, who tended to the boiling pot. I made short work of my chunk of bread, and took my time over my coffee. With both hands cupped around the metal mug, I felt at peace. Relaxed, almost sedate. The rising warmth of the house was making me drowsy. We didn't have a fire going, since that could give us away, but just being indoors again felt very cosy. I hoped to get some sleep very soon, since I needed it that was for sure. My weapons needed cleaning first before I turned in, I couldn't neglect them any more than I already had. Thomas opened the conversation.

'We need to prepare to relocate back towards Detmold.' Detmold wasn't too far from here. About six kilometres away to the north. Thomas continued.

'That roadblock has served its purpose. No point wasting lives back up there now. If I was a betting man, they will crucify it with artillery tomorrow before they venture back up there.'

My thoughts turned to the American they had staked to it. Did that tank crew even know he was there?

'The Americans will be in Berlebeck soon', Thomas stated, 'mark my words, all we can do is play for time, and punish them when and where we can.'

Eating men nodded their agreement. Everyone clearly felt the same. Nothing more was really said at the table. We all had experienced a long day, and we were just filling our bellies before we took a well needed rest. Once we had our fill, some got out of their seats and made their way into the cellar. Before I could turn in, I was instructed to go upstairs and relieve Johann so he could come and eat. I was so tired I didn't have the strength, or the courage to protest. We were all tired. I quickly shuffled down into the cellar to grab some rag and weapon oil so I could tend to my filthy MP40 whilst up there. I ensured I had all my fighting gear with me, should the Americans be rude enough to turn up whilst I was up there. I made my way up to the bedroom cum sentry position. Johann was very grateful for me taking over, since he was ravenous, and could do with some coffee too. He took his weapons and belt kit with him, leaving me to peer out into the gardens from behind the thin netting. I chose to remain standing whilst I cleaned my weapon, the temptation to sit and close my eyes was becoming far too much of an alluring prospect. Ensuring that the weapon was completely unloaded, I went about stripping it down to it basic component parts. The part that took the longest was scraping all the mud and crap off of the body. Once I had achieved that, I then inspected it carefully for rust and damage. It didn't look like it was damaged, but there was some rust at various points along the welds and fittings. I didn't have anything abrasive to remove it, but I was sure it wouldn't affect its performance when or if I needed to use it again. I applied a generous amount of weapon oil over all the metal bearing surfaces, working parts, along with the outside of the entire weapon. The oil would take care of the carbon that had built up on some of the moving parts, again with no abrasive to remove it, it would have to do. The oil would also prevent any further onset of rust on the weapon. I then rebuilt the weapon, ensuring before I replaced the magazine, the firing mechanism worked. It worked just fine.

The magazine was looking sorry for itself too, so I fitted a fresh clean magazine to the weapon before emptying and stripping it. I needed the weapon ready for action. I unloaded the magazine of its rounds, inspecting each one in the palm of my hand, giving them a thorough wipe over with a clean rag. Once the ammunition was dealt with, I then removed the spring from the magazine body, and gave them both a real good wipe down with the same rag. I rebuilt the magazine, ensuring the spring still had some life in it, and would chamber the rounds without causing a stoppage. That's the last thing you need in a fight, the bloody thing not firing. Once content the magazine was serviceable, I then fed the magazine its' rounds and placed it away in my magazine pouch upside down. You don't want to lose ammunition when you are dashing and diving about.

I remained standing during my duty. I would only fall asleep if I sat down. I would close my eyes for what I felt was just a moment, and I would shock myself awake as my knees buckled. I could hear the thud of boots coming up the stairs. I turned to see Lars in the doorway. Was my duty over already? Lars was full of smile, and not only armed with weapons, but a pot of coffee and two mugs. Please just let me sleep!

'Thought you could do with some company, and some of this stuff to keep you awake.' He offered me and empty cup.

'Thank you, I am shattered!' I croaked. He nodded in agreement.

'I know how you feel, I'm ready for bed, but we need two people on through the night at any one time.'

He put the pot and his cup on the nearest bedside dresser, and began to carefully remove various items from a large set of drawers. He carefully placed them on the floor in the far corner of the room.

'I'm not one for wrecking peoples' property'. He beamed,' I would be very pissed off if any of our soldiers trashed my house.'

Such rare compassion in these times of madness.

He then dragged the unit into the middle of the room, and then put his weapons beneath the window frame on the floor. All very familiar. Borchen felt like a lifetime ago. He then poured us both a coffee and invited me to join him, sat on the rather spacious set of drawers. We sat in relative comfort, and could see out into the gardens. Why didn't I think of that?

I enjoyed my coffee. It gave me something to do. It was strong too. It certainly took the edge off my tiredness. A polite silence hung in the air, which was both comfortable, but at the same time awkward. Lars took the lead.

'So young Erik, after the war, will you stay in the SS?'

I wasn't too sure how to really deal with this question, without sounding out of turn.

'Well that depends.'

Lars took another sip of his coffee, 'on what?'

I was nervous, but I had put myself in a fucking corner already, I swallowed hard.

'If we win.'

Out of the corner of my right eye, I could see Lars taking interest in whatever was at the bottom of his cup. Was he up here to test my loyalty? Had I already failed? Was I now one of many defeatists that now riddled this shattered nation? Without looking up from his cup, he pushed.

'What makes you think we are losing?'

I wished I was on duty by myself again. I could see this conversation going bad. Lars turned to look at me, not menacing, just stern.

'Well?' he pushed.

I took a deep breath, 'may I speak freely?'

Lars kept a stern fix on me and slowly nodded. Here goes.

'The Russians are very close to Berlin. We happen to be fighting the Americans. I don't know where the British and Canadians are. We hung a girl because she was talking to the Americans. We crucified a prisoner at the roadblock, and I'm not sure if we are on a winning streak right now. Everything is getting more spiteful, more wicked. I fought the Americans at Borchen not too long ago, and that felt like more like, shall we say a fair fight.'

I knew I had said too much, it was time for me to shut the fuck up.

Lars' demeanour relaxed, and nodded, 'you are a bright kid Erik, I'll give you that. Desperate times call for desperate measures, more coffee?'

Coffee? I felt I was about to be shot for being defeatist. 'Am I in trouble?'

Lars looked at me with a puzzled expression, 'for what? Knowing when the chips are down? Erik, I'm too long in the tooth to really give a damn about the misgivings of the German people, I just won't allow the invaders to relax and enjoy the spoils our country offer. You are just a boy, enjoy being just that. There are too many men fucking this whole situation up as it is, regardless of their reservations.' He broke into a friendly grin,' enjoy the war Erik, that's all that matters right now.'

I thought of Bobby, he just wanted to survive the war, and go home.

I want to go home.

The remainder of our time was filled with plenty of coffee and little chit chat. Lars was from Dortmund, a huge industrial city. Now in American hands. He had no idea if his family was safe or not. He lived for the fight, since that's all he had to call living right now. He was not interested in surrendering. The Americans hated the SS, which was no secret. Lars had escaped from the freezing Ardennes with literally his life and what he was wearing earlier this year. His unit was chewed up by just sheer weight of American firepower. He had an axe to grind with them that was for sure.

It was dark by the time our sentry duty had ended. Lars told me to go into the cellar and give Otto and Viktor a shove, since it was their turn. I gathered up all my equipment, and made my way downstairs. The stairs that led down into the basement creaked and groaned, as I tried to be as quite as possible. In the soft light of oil lamps, I could make out Thomas' profile as he sat at the table with the radio set on. The speaker crackled as a very grainy voice was giving instructions on how to use a panzerfaust. What type of radio station was this? It certainly wasn't Lilly Marlene.

'Who is that broadcasting?' I whispered.

'The Reich Minister', Thomas informed me. 'He runs a feature called 'Radio Werewolf'.

'What is Radio Werewolf?' This was rather bizarre. Thomas continued to speak without looking at me.

'It calls for the German nation to rise up and fight the invaders. Demanding that every man, woman and child take up arms and defend the Reich. And to destroy those who collaborate with them. The people receive instructions on how to use certain weapons throughout the broadcast.'

'Radio Werewolf' must have been ordered by the Fuhrer. There must be millions of weapons all over the country right now for citizens to use. So we are losing. Why else would the citizens have to fight? The end to this war must be near. I had one question on my lips.

'Are we Werewolves?' I whispered.

Thomas turned and fixed a relaxed gaze on me. 'Aren't you supposed to be waking up your relief Erik?'

'Err, yes, sorry to pester you.' I stammered. Thomas gave me a warm smile.

'You need to rest, boy. You've had some crazy adventures recently.'

I nodded in agreement as I backed away. I felt like a persistent child that didn't know when to be quiet. There were a lot of empty cot beds, as I tried to find Otto and Viktor in the dull lamp glow. It wasn't long when I found them, giving them a gentle nudged. I waited impatiently for them to rise. I didn't want them to fall back asleep, since I craved for my own. The typical soldiers' chorus of coughs and farts filled the dark, stuffy cellar for a few minutes. Other sleeping soldiers disturbed by these two getting out of bed threatened them with slow and violent deaths if they didn't shut up. The usual banter of a barracks, nothing ever changes. I remained on my feet as they gathered their gear and weapons and stumbled clumsily upstairs. They were exhausted, but it was their turn on sentry duty. I found myself an empty cot now void of an owner. I think it was Gerhard's'. I missed that man. He was a nice guy. I didn't know too much about his recent exploits during the war, nor did I really care. I liked him. I pulled my boots off. It felt amazing to get them bloody things off. The smell that came with it didn't smell too ripe, but I could live with that. I removed my muddy, tunic, and dropped it to the floor. I laid my weapons and equipment under where my arse pushed a dent in the tight canvas of the cot. I had two blankets', one I folded into a crude pillow; the other would be my cover.

As I lay down, the heavy steps of Lars thudded and creaked down the cellar steps. He stopped to chat to Thomas. Instantly, I fretted over him telling Thomas about our conversation upstairs. I relaxed slightly when they both appeared to chuckle, and not in a menacing way either, just light amusement. Maybe the two oafs that staggered upstairs had caused them to find something funny? I put the full weight of my head onto my makeshift pillow. The last thing I could hear as I faded was someone teaching the nation how to use an MG42.

## 11.

Heavy boots on the floor above.

Heavy boots on creaking stairs.

Raised, angry voices.

Furniture being tossed aside.

My world exploded to life, as I crashed to the hard stone floor face first. Had I fallen out of bed? I turned onto my back, and as my world came into focus, my heart jumped into my throat.

Above me, filthy, bloodied, and angry, stood Dieter.

'You weak, spineless little shit.' He snarled.

Before I could find words to say, he reached down, grabbed me by my shirt and groin and dragged me up, shoving me heavily against the cellar wall. All the wind was knocked out of me; I was seeing sparkles, as I fought to fill my lungs with air.

I wasn't dreaming Dieter was very much real; the burning sensation in my stomach due to him having me by my balls was very real too.

'What's going on here?' demanded Thomas over the commotion of the others scrambling out of their cots to gather around us.

Dieter continued to snarl at me, through gritted teeth.

'This little shit deserted us in the face of the enemy. He ran away!' he roared, throwing me to the floor. I landed heavily on my left side, winded once more. I curled up, expecting the angry giant to put the boot in. It never came. Thomas stepped forward in front of the furious Dieter, glaring at me as he now stood over me.

'Is this true?' Thomas barked, 'did you run away from battle?'

I looked up, still trying to draw in breath. Both Thomas and Dieter stood over me, faces full of anger. Dieter went for me again, this time Thomas held him off.

'Let him speak!' Thomas commanded. I always thought Dieter was the leader; it would appear that Thomas was taking the lead, since we all thought Dieter was dead up till now. I managed to get my words out.

'Dieter charged the enemy, whilst I tended to Gerhard, who was wounded.' I forced out.' Anton and Konrad followed him into the attack; Gerhard was in a bad way.'

They looked no less angry, but they remained where they stood. The remainder of the group looked at Dieter and each other. No one wanted to make the first move. Thomas took a sudden step forward, which made me flinch. He squatted down, and looked me straight in the eyes.

'Listen to me boy', in a soft but stern tone of voice.' In the heat of battle, you leave the wounded where they fall, do you understand?'

'Yes Sir!' I responded instantly, trying not to well up.

Thomas looked me up and down, with a slow nod. He rose to his feet, and turned to face Dieter, addressing the group as a collective.

'The boy will not let any of us down again; he tended to a wounded comrade. He is not hardened to our expectations as of yet. My one to one class yesterday with him has hopefully purged some of his youthful weakness from him.' He turned to look down at me, and summoned me to get up.

I clambered to my feet, wiping my tears from my filthy face. The group all nodded independently and went about their business. Thomas gave me a firm grip on my shoulder and then made his way back to the radio set. I was left alone with the monster that was Dieter stood over me. He gave me a rough shove against the wall, which I was ready for, so I wasn't winded on this occasion. As he turned to walk away, a phrase I never wanted to hear whilst in this cellar roared out above us.

'American infantry!'

The house suddenly vibrated with the familiar rippling bursts of MG42. Those who had gone back to bed sprung up like they had just received an electric shock. We frantically scrambled for boots, and weapons. Those already dressed stampeded up the cellar stairs, when a huge thud rocked the house, causing dust and timber splinters from above to rain down on us. Those caught on the stairs came crashing back down on top of each other.

'Panzershrek' came the roar upstairs. The Americans had their own version. One of which had clearly just hit the house somewhere. As those in the pile at the bottom of the stairs untangled themselves, another rocket hit the floors above, resulting in a louder thud that sent ears ringing, especially mine. As the soundtrack of ambushed men came rushing back into my head, I had finally got my boots on and my weapons in my hands. I looked up and saw Thomas stood at the radio table pointing his MP40 at Dieter who was trying to get upstairs.

'You are a fucking arsehole!' Thomas roared over the dreadful din of gunfire and shouting up in the kitchen. 'You led them here!'

Dieter, as big and as terrifying as he could be on a good day did not contest the allegation, he fought his way upstairs to take on our attackers. Thomas' glare then fixed on me. I dared not move; maybe we had led them to the house, allowing Dieter to come through unmolested. He flicked his head towards the stair case. I quickly complied and staggered up the stairs.

I crawled into the kitchen on my hands and knees. The noise was incredible. Viktor and Otto were fighting it out with whoever was just outside the kitchen window and the door to the gardens. Their disciplined single shots of their MP40s' were no match for the colossal firepower coming from the Americans. The snaps of incoming rounds were just a constant din, which was systematically disintegrating the kitchen and its fittings. Units splintered, glass cracked, crockery burst all over the room. I felt a jab of weapon muzzle on my right buttock. I peered around, Thomas was glaring at me, face full of fury.

'Get your fucking arse out of the way you fool, get to where you can fight!' he roared above the din.

The kitchen was slowly becoming untenable, even for Viktor and Otto. I scrambled and slipped on the wet tiles out into the room next to it. Life was short if anyone stood up. Rounds snapped through, wall fittings burst all over us, the blackout material was in shreds, yet it continued to flick and dance as enemy fire poured in. I crawled over to one of the windows; my intention was to fight from it. Just a few feet short, the lower half of the window frame splintered and collapsed, which caused the entire frame, and all that was attached to it to fall in, crashing down over the top of me. The weight of the frame, curtains, and the majority of the glass stunned me as it took my breath. I was pinned to the floor. The snap of incoming fire grew more intense. The Americans now had an entry point into the house. With me at the entrance. I had to get out of the way at least. I put the palms of my hands on the splintered and glass littered floor and began to push up. The window frame began to shift; it wasn't too heavy, just fucking awkward.

Suddenly the frame doubled in weight, and I was pinned to the floor once more. The chattering of automatic fire directly above my head had my ears ringing once more. Hot brass hit the back of my head and neck. Searing hot, I tried to get my hands up to brush the red hot brass away from my skin. Once the gunfire ceased, my call out for help was muffled due to my lack of hearing. The weight across my back lightened almost instantly, and the frame was lifted from my body. When I had enough room, I spun around. Otto was stood over me, heaving the smashed window frame up and over so I could get free.

'Don't just fucking lay there boy, get out of the fucking way!' Roared Otto.

I crawled back away from the large hole that once held the frame, between Otto's' legs and then got into a kneeling position. Once the frame was dealt with, Otto reached out for my shirt, and dragged me back towards the door that joined both this room and the kitchen. The kitchen was a wreck. The table was shattered; just behind it Viktor was slumped against the unit just beneath the sink. His eyes were still open, but there was no life in his eyes. His blood hung like a spider web all over the cupboard door. Otto clipped me around the head.

'We cannot stay here!' he roared in my ear. Upstairs, whoever was manning the MG42s' was still firing short, controlled bursts.' We need to get back to Detmold somehow!'

It was broad daylight outside; fighting our way through the Americans would be nothing short of suicide. But if we stayed here, we would die. Another jarring thud hit the house. The Americans were throwing everything at us. Had they got armour around the roadblock? Or had they just walked in on Dieters trail, carrying their own rockets? Outside, I could just make out a rather strange, long roar. Then another. I could now smell gasoline and burning wood.

'Flame Thrower!' screamed someone upstairs.

The look of horror on Otto's' face was something I would never forget. Another long roar of gasoline swept through the house. I coughed and spluttered as it took all the air from the house. The sudden lack of air made me feel very ill and light headed. Upstairs, the once short controlled bursts of machine gun fire were now long and desperate. Desperate men struggling to deal with the flame thrower menace. With each roar of flame and overwhelming aroma of gasoline, came a horrendous amount of incoming fire. The Americans were protecting their best weapon, no doubt about it.

Our own machine gun fire suddenly ceased, replaced instantly by hysterical screaming. Otto waved for me to follow him. On our hands and knees we scrambled through the room with the caved in window, and into an adjoining corridor with staircase going up. Smoke billowed from the upstairs rooms. The upstairs landing was thick with smoke. A screaming mass of flame came running out of the upper right room, and crashed into the banister, sending it tumbling down the staircase, leaving clusters of flaming gasoline all over the stair case. It was one of the gunners. His screams went right through me. He hit the lower floor with such force, I heard bones crunch amid his screams. He spun around on the floor, like he was wrestling a crocodile or something, his screams becoming higher pitched. When I thought my ears couldn't take any more, there was a loud, sharp snap, instantly rending the human torch perfectly still. It was only then I noticed the smoking Luger in Otto's' hand. I was stunned beyond words. I knew why he had done it, but you never think it will ever happen in your lifetime.

'Let's get out of here!' he bellowed over the constant incoming snaps that were dismantling the stair case.

I followed him in a lower crawl back to where he had lifted the window from off of me. As he peered outside, I could hear foreign voices echoing through the kitchen. Enemy troops were now entering the house. They would not take pity on us. We had to flee.

'Now!' he hissed as he leaped to his feet. Scrambling out of the opening. I didn't wait to be told again. I got through the opening, and made off after him, he was sprinting like a mad man for a log pile in an adjoining garden. We had got about half way, when I heard shouting and commotion from the house. Multiple snaps cracked passed us, splintering the log pile as we dashed towards it. Otto's' torso burst in a fine red mist, causing him to crash to the floor face first. I put more effort into my sprint, my lungs fit to burst, and the snaps became more intense. Tracer rounds flicked off the log pile smashing into a house nearby. I slid in behind the logs, hugging the floor, lungs burning, dragging in air like it was my last. The incoming fire thudded constantly into the log pile, which to my relief was fairly high, and wide at its base. Tracer had set fire to the neighbouring roof. I was a heaving sweaty mess, in just a shirt, boots and trousers. I had no weapons to defend myself. All I could do right now was sit tight and pray the Americans wouldn't pursue me. The incoming fire lifted fairly quickly. The only snapping and crackling now was the burning roof next to me. I couldn't stay there, that was for sure. I got up into the kneeling position and slowly moved back away from the log pile. Just over the top of it, I could just make out the rising smoke column that was once our house. I slowly raised myself up to get a better view. The house was now just a raging inferno. I knelt back down and turned my back on the pile. I needed to get out of there and keep out of line of sight of the house for as long as I could. Between me and the other end of Berlebeck was the main road, and various dwellings and out buildings. The wire strand fences could slow me down, but I would just have to dive over them. I made a short sharp dash behind the house next to me. Its roof fire had really taken hold now. Maybe the smoke it was generating would work in my favour.

I made a bold dash to the road, just as I hit the cobbles, the stream that ran alongside offered some cover, but not enough. I was now committed to crossing the road, dreading incoming fire. I was, yet again a heaving, lung burning mess by the time I'd made it to the cluster of houses on the other side. On the plus side though, there was a lot more cover over there. Once I had composed myself, I peered to look back at the route I had taken. Our house was well and truly ablaze. As for the other house, next to the log pile, the roof had now collapsed in to the main building. I just hoped no one was home.

I couldn't stay there for too long. I couldn't see any Americans around the burning houses, but that didn't mean they weren't still in the area. Maybe our encounter with them this morning was deliberate. A revenge attack for both the girl and their guy we nailed to the logs. Or were they advancing towards Detmold? Detmold was about six kilometres to the north of here. I'm sure I could make it there once it got dark. The question is, what do I do when I got there? The locals may report me to the Military Police. The Americans could already be there. I didn't know of any family or friends of my mother living there. They would probably prefer not to assist than harbour a deserter. The authorities would be just as harsh on them should I be discovered in their care. There was a lot to risk, but to be fair, just living around here right now was risky. It quickly dawned on me, that since my first venture into this village, I hadn't seen anyone. Was Berlebeck abandoned? Or did the locals just hide in their cellars? Besides the roaring and crackling of the burning buildings, there was nothing going on.

I wouldn't make my move to Detmold until it got dark. Bearing in mind the time of year, I wouldn't have to wait too long. I was bloody cold though. I kept the cold at bay by constantly moving from house to house, trying to see if any of the enemy was still in the area. As the cold day wore on, the more I was convinced that they deliberately came just to destroy us. They had no need to sit in Berlebeck longer than they had to. Thankfully, by mid afternoon, the light started to fade, yet the wind picked up, adding to my misery. I had to get moving soon. The sooner I got into Detmold, the sooner I could get food and warm clothing. I had to make up my mind whether to go through gardens and farmland or stick to the roads. I had no map, so going through the fields could lead me to god knows where, but if I kept to the roads, would Military Police pick me up at a check point? Labelled as a deserter, I would sooner take my chances with the Americans, than our own side. Yes the Americans could shoot me, but to be arrested by my own wasn't worth even considering. If what we did to the girl was anything to go by, Germany was in no mood to tolerate weak and defeatist people right now.

I couldn't stand the hanging around any longer. I set off north out of Berlebeck hopefully in the right direction to Detmold. I would take my chances on the roads. If anything looked like a patrol, enemy or otherwise, I would just go to ground until it passed. That's all I could do right now. I walked on the road until I was clear of the village. Once into the lanes that led me out, it was difficult to get away from the road. High hedgerows and deep long ditches either side made progress slow. I was losing light a lot faster than I'd expected, the spindly branches of the canopy closed in, stealing the light. Every now and then, the hedgerows would end, and open up to large gardens of chicken runs and wire strand fences. They slowed me down, but at least I could get away from the road for a little while. Little houses dotted the landscape. No lights, maybe just a light grey plume of smoke from a chimney indicated they were occupied. I would flinch every time a chicken would cluck loudly as I passed its little wooden house. I was hungry, but taking care of one of them chickens was more trouble than it was worth. The racket it would make as I tried to grab it and kill it would wake half of the neighbourhood. Then I would have to carry it with me, and try to cook the thing once I found somewhere suitable. I think the last time I had meat to eat was on the Senne, and that felt like a lifetime ago. My mind wandered to our classroom instruction, a log fire roaring as the snow fell outside. The warm barrack block with its log fire stove. And now look at me, in the back of beyond in just a fucking shirt, freezing my arse off.

Max was firm but fair as instructors went. He didn't dazzle us with all that propaganda that the officers would lead you to believe. He would tell you exactly what combat was like, against both the British and the Russians. In France he said that the British were good fighters, but painfully slow and cautious. Many a time, his unit would get bored of waiting and take the initiative and attack them as they carefully got their people into position. The Russians however were a totally different enemy. Extremely aggressive, and mob handed. They would throw unit after unit at any German units facing them. Killing them wasn't the problem, according to Max; it was having enough ammunition to kill all of them. It was his tank killing prowess that got him assigned to the Senne as an instructor. Wounded in both France and Russia, he recovered sufficiently enough to pass his knowledge on to us. I bet the last thing he planned for was to be in the middle of a lesson one day and then receiving orders to march just south of Paderborn to fight with his students. To be brutally honest with myself, if it wasn't for what Max had taught me during my time at the Senne, let alone what he taught me in the few hours before his death, I could very well be dead myself.

The open ground began to fall away to the right, away from the road. The wire fences were a pain in the arse, every time I tried to be quiet as I clambered over, they would flick like a violin string further down. It wasn't long before I was in a shallow valley of sorts, with the road on the high ground to my left. There was no traffic to be seen nor heard, but I was glad to be away from it all the same. It reduced the chances of me running into a check point of ours. The clouds began to part, and the moon lit up the whole area considerably. Navigation became easier, and I could anticipate the wire fences easier and skirt around them. The only dilemma I had now was progress. With all my detours around fence lines I wasn't getting any bloody closer to Detmold. The clear night made me all the more colder. My shirt had now dried to a certain extent, but it didn't keep out
the cold. The temptation to seek refuge in one of the houses before me was becoming all the more alluring, but the last time I broke into a house, I ended up with a load of SS deserters, claiming to do the Reichfuhrers' bidding. As far as I was now concerned, they were just a bunch of thugs trying to justify their existence. Some were likeable, let it be said, but they all had the same twisted idea of what was going to happen to Germany once this war was over.

Before long, I was fighting my way through small gardens, with more dogs barking away, chickens and other livestock making silly noises. It must have been deemed as normal around here for such a racket, since no one came out to investigate. I ended up on a loose gravel track. I tried to be as quiet as possible in my boots but it was difficult. The track must have taken me about two hundred metres or so when it brought me out onto a main road. Not what I had planned, but then again, I was losing all sense of direction in the maze of gardens, the road could help me reset my mental compass. I had clearly drifted back towards the main road somehow. Oh well, I chose to walk on it until the ground allowed me to get off it once more. The road twisted and turned. The bends were a long shallow bend, so I would carefully pace my way around the long corner so I didn't stumble into civilians, who could give me away, or bump into soldiers of either side. Either way it could end badly for me. Once I had traversed my way around one particular bend, I noticed a road sign up ahead. I could make out what was on it until I'd gotten right up to it. My heart sank.

'Welcome to Horn'

I so nearly cursed out load. Erik you fucking idiot, you are on the wrong road! The road I had discovered at the end of the track was another road branching off from the Detmold road. I now knew where I was, and it was nowhere near fucking Detmold. In the grand scheme of things, I had almost walked in a huge circle. If I followed the road out of Horn to the right it would take me through Kohlstadt and back to Schlangen. Not good. There was only one thing to do now. Get into Horn and rest, then tomorrow night try for Detmold again. I could feel myself getting all silly and emotional. I just wanted to eat rest and get warm. I just wanted to find a little place where I could just sit, and let the war pass me by. Call me a coward if you want, but it couldn't be much longer now before this madness would finally end.

Horn was a much more cluttered village than Berlebeck. The houses almost sat on top of each other. No vast gardens to hide in. Plenty of damp log piles and the like, but remaining hidden here was going to be difficult, I could feel it. A long roadside ditch opened up to my right, and I happily clambered into it. There appeared to be a lot of people and vehicle traffic up a head. My stomach flipped. I hoped it wasn't a check point. I could hear shouting and cursing. As I slowly drew closer, I recognised it as German. Soldiers? SS? Police? The engine noise roared and along with it, the unmistakable clattering of tracks. There was armour in Horn. To my right there was a group of houses scattered about a small hill of sorts. I got out of the ditch, and made my way into the gardens. I did not want to get captured in the check point. In this darkness, it could be shoot first, check the body after. I carefully negotiated the gardens and made my way to the top of this hill. It wasn't that big, but I had a decent view of what was going on the other side.

Panzers, lots of them. Parked up almost nose to tail. Their crews were either on them, or walking around them. The crews sat on them appeared very relaxed, smoking away; one of them appeared to be playing an accordion. I found this most alarming. The Americans could very well be in the woods around here, you just couldn't tell. The hill I was sat on was covered in thick trees, which gave me an element of cover. I took the time to carefully scan the woods between me and the road for any of their sentries. I couldn't see any. To my right, the hill sloped away down towards the road. I needed to find somewhere to stay through the day without detection. Before I went looking for refuge, I needed to pee. Confident in my surroundings, I turned my back on the road and went about my business. I didn't have much to give, since I'd not eaten properly or drank anything for a while.

'Hey you!' came a shout behind me. My whole world had just collapsed.

'Hello, you in the shirt' I dared not move. I could hear the crunch of leaf litter getting closer.

I spun around; I was face to face with a soldier in full gear, and a torch.

'What are you playing at?' demanded the soldier.

Playing at? I had no idea what he was suggesting. Any possible explanation just poured out of my ears. I just had to front it out.

'I'm taking a piss!' I boldly stated.

'Don't get funny with me you scruffy buffoon!' barked the sentry; 'the Hauptmann's' orders are that all crew are correctly dressed when away from their panzers'.

Hauptmann? This must have been an Army unit; their rank structure was different to ours.

'Oh, right. Sorry.' I just couldn't think of anything else.

With a wave of his torch, he waved me down to the road. 'Get back to your vehicle, don't fuck up again, understand?'

The chance of me making a run for it was well and truly gone. Should I have done so, this Army unit would be out in force looking for one of their scruffy number wearing just a shirt. My mind was racing, how the hell was I going to get out of this one? I came down the hill, the sentry glaring at me all the way. He wasn't a threat to me, since he thought I was just one of the many scruffy panzer crewmen in his unit. Just before the road was another ditch that ran alongside. A jumped across and then made myself remotely presentable, tucking my shirt in properly, even ensuring my braces were over my shoulders. I ran my fingers through my hair, and set my eyes on the crew lounging all over a Panther about ten meters in front of me. What the hell was I going to say to them? Hi I'm Erik, I'm from the SS and looking to Join your crew. If they didn't beat me up on the spot just for being SS that would be a miracle. The Army and SS have never got on. Not too sure why, just a real professional rivalry. I had to play for time, I couldn't just climb on any vehicle, tank crews are like families, and you can't just hide in their numbers. I decided to stroll up the column to my right. The moon had the whole area fairly well lit. I just hoped it was dark enough me to buy sometime and think of something.

As I strolled up the column, I could see a crowd gathering up ahead of me. Then, members of this crowd called out.

'Everyone, get up here!' came the shout down the line.

Oh shit.

I eased off my confident stride and tried to think of a way I could get around the vehicles and vanish. What the hell was I going to do? At this stage, I wasn't confident about my chances if they discovered an imposter amongst them. It may cause a laugh to see the SS in a bad way, or it could spark outrage and a lynch mob. Just next to me and also in front, panzers crews were clambering down from their vehicles, the waft of tobacco smelt amazing. Farts and coffee breath soon mixed in with the aroma of unwashed men. I now found myself in amongst a loose crowd. I could hear the gallop of boots behind me as other tank crews caught up with our group. Darkness would only be my friend for so long, since it would soon be a new day. What that day would bring was anyone's' guess. I was now in the middle of a large group of strangers. Any fear of the situation suddenly evaporated. If I aroused suspicion, I would introduce myself to their commander, who hopefully would keep the mob at bay. After all, they would want every man capable of fighting surely?

Our crowd drew up just in front what appeared to be a group of officers. Even in the low light we were all immersed in, I could tell all was not well. Some were sobbing, quiet openly. Others had their back to us, hands on hips, looking up at the dark sky, shaking their heads. The only one who looking unfazed by what was happening around him was the one in the middle, slowly and carefully folding up his map. He invited us all to smoke with him, since he wanted to address us.

The officer himself rolled a cigarette, the glow of his match gave away that he had not shaven in a while. I carefully scanned about me; it was evident that most of his unit hadn't shaved in a while either. I didn't feel so scruffy now. He then asked his men to sit down where they could. Most just slumped in the middle of the road. I too squatted down, carefully making contact with both gravel and buttocks. The officers remained standing. I peered around; some of the more grizzled veterans who must have been NCO's remained stood at the rear of the group. The officer cleared his throat.

'Gentlemen, it appears that events have overtaken us in a way I never ever once considered.'

He paused, the odd cough and fart emitted from the group around me.

'Germany is in trouble. Real trouble. By rights I should keep you focused on your mission to fight for your Fuhrer, your Fatherland, your way of life. I feel that to do so, I would be nothing but a fraud.'

Mutters and murmurs slowly built up in the group. He held out his hands for calm.

'I must now be open and frank with you. Not as your Commanding Officer, but as a fellow man caught up in these circumstances that we are party to. When I took command of this unit just prior to Poland, it was one of the greatest feelings In my entire life, second only to the birth of my children. I felt invincible. Poland, Belgium, Holland, France, I felt as if nothing could stop my boys.'

I could tell he was starting to well up. He composed himself well, cleared his throat, and carried on.

'And then there was Russia. Russia beat up my unit really bad. A lot of good boys were lost in Russia, and if I was brutally honest with you, it gave me sleepless nights. I began to live in fear of losing more the next day for more land than any man could possibly want. Kursk almost cost me my unit. Our losses were horrendous. The powers that be saw fit to return us to France for rest and refitting, and I won't lie to you men, that was some of the greatest news I had heard in a while.'

He was trying his hardest not to break down. Even some of the hard faced NCOs' were putting up a good fight with the tears.

'Last year turned out to be the bloodiest year I have ever witnessed. Normandy was a tough fight, but we managed to get out of France. The Hurtgen Wald is where most of you sat before me cut your teeth. I'm proud to say you guys gave a good account of yourselves there. We struggled to get fuel and spares, but we made it work. I am eternally grateful for the job you did in the Hurtgen.'

Various nods and shoulder patting amongst those sat in front of me.

'Now let's talk about where we are now. We have no fuel, no spares, and little if any ammunition. We have not had contact with Command for some time now. We know that there is a substantial American force in Paderborn, and up north towards Minden, there are British units pushing east. So as you can guess, we are in a bit of a fix. I have spoken to my officers just a few minutes ago, and I have made it clear that I will not order you into a fight with the odds stacked against us anymore. As of now, my obligation to you is to see that you leave the battlefield alive. As of now you are free to return to your homes, or find other units in the area. You have served your country, and served it well. Now I must, as an officer, and as a man endeavour to save your lives, for I have lost enough since 1939, enough is enough.'

There was stunned silence in the group. I was stunned. Never did I think I would hear one of our officers speak this way. What a bizarre feeling. We could walk away now, without reprisal. The officer cleared his throat, wiping away his tears as he did so.

'Sentries! I would be eternally grateful if you did not shoot any member of my unit who wish to leave. Thank you.'

He looked over us, eyes glazed, and a broad, warm smile on his face.

'Go home boys, go home. Consider a handshake with your former Commanding Officer the end of your contract.'

With that he walked over to the front of the vehicle column, and rolled himself another cigarette. His officers slowly made their way towards him. Some joined him in a smoke; others just stood there, hands in pockets, playing with the gravel beneath their boot. He shook the hands of his officers, at which point some burst into tears, thanking him for letting them go home. This whole situation was totally bizarre. A unit disbanded in the field. Would the SS do such a thing? Probably not. The lads around me slowly got to their feet, some clearly tearful. Many shook hands; others remained seated, totally numb by what had just taken place.

We could all go home.

I kept myself to myself as the boys around me, mostly young; some old embraced each other, sobbing openly. This truly was a wonderful day for these guys. Their war as far as fighting was concerned was over. Their next risky adventure was getting home. For most, it would be difficult, for some it would end in heartbreak. Their families were fighting the war as well. Those boys from the cities knew the enemy had destroyed most of the big towns and cities. God only knew what they would find upon their return. They would have to brave the Military Police checkpoints, and any other units who would be on their path home. And then there was the enemy. Getting rounded up as prisoners was a real possibility too. The real adventure was about to begin for them, getting home. Did they go home armed? Since they may need to defend themselves. Or did they lay down their arms and take their chances? It was still all to play for.

There was not the mass exodus from the column I had first thought. Most of the boys went back to their tanks, probably to contemplate the long journey home. I felt for those who were from the east. Their home towns overrun by the Russians. As for the Americans and the British, I guess you had to catch them on a good day. There were no weapons left on the road, they had taken them back to their vehicles. Some old habits would forever die hard. The men, as scruffy as they appeared, kept their column immaculate. The boys appeared in no rush to leave. They lounged about on their tanks, smoking, laughing, and singing along to the accordion. I felt the presence of someone next to me. I turned to see their Commanding Officer.

'They are good boys; I just couldn't send them to their deaths anymore.' He muttered as he let out a long pillar of cigarette smoke. I was bang to rights at that point, I just played along.

'Yes Sir.'

He turned to look at me, he wasn't particularly tall. In the growing light of dawn, I could see his dark hair swept back, his face carrying several days of beard. He was handsome, but with a piercing confident glare you would expect from an officer in the Wehrmacht.

'I know almost all of my men, but I'm afraid you have me at a loss young man, I'm Erik Wrobel' he held out his hand, with a beaming smile to go with it.

I accepted his hand,' Erik Baum, Sir.'

His grip was firm, very firm. 'Handsome name there Erik, your parents made a great choice.'

I accepted his compliment; he released his grip, the blood washed back into my hand.

'Where are you from young Erik?' he enquired.

'Paderborn Sir, Bad Lipspringge.'

He nodded slowly, 'I didn't know we had any Paderborn boys in the unit.' I felt fear flood through me suddenly. 'I'm surprised you were not recruited into the SS.'

I did not want to betray a man who had just allowed his men to go home, so I came clean.

'Sir, my unit was destroyed just south of Kohlstadt but a few days ago. I have been evading the Americans since, and I stumbled across your unit quiet by accident this morning.'

He crossed his arms, and stroked his beard. 'So that would be the tank fire we heard just the other day.' He concluded. 'My initial orders were to link up with an SS outfit just south of here, but you SS guys can be a prickly bunch to work with let it be said. We were so low on fuel and ammunition; I decided not to link up and commit my boys to a blood bath. I'm sure you understand.'

Wrobels' was the unit sent to reinforce us. My thoughts filled with that of Max, Bobby, and Marco.

I nodded, 'Sir, doing that one act has saved the lives of so many of these guys. The Americans threw everything at us; it would have been a waste of life.'

He continued to nod as he stroked his beard.' Agreed, at least these boys can go home now, I'm tired Erik, we are merely playing for time now. How many more have to die before it all stops?'

I swallowed hard, and had to ask him. 'Sir, may I go home too?'

He turned, looking me straight in the eyes.' My young Erik, even the SS have mothers, so I'm told.'

His cheeky wink reassured me I was not about to be handed over to another unit. 'Go home, but be cautious, the Americans are a prickly bunch too. Very unpredictable, take it from me.'

The feeling of joy rose up in me to a point, where I could feel my eyes flooding. I shook his hand vigorously with both hands, 'thank you Sir thank you.'

I could now go home.

## 12.

Despite being told that they were free to go home, none of the men appeared to be in a rush to go. They continued to lounge about on their vehicles, singing songs, smoking, drinking coffee. It was almost a feeling of being too proud to be the first one to shake the Commanding Officers' hand and walk away. Maybe as far as they were concerned, they were home. These guys, by the looks of them had been to hell and back just to see how far it was, together. I watched one particular crew, the eldest one, who no doubt was the panzer commander, almost played mother hen to his crew, his children in a sense. He was the one refilling their coffee cups, relighting their cigarettes, since playing cards was the main activity up on the turret. Looking at the other crews, some just lazed where they could, smoking, some reading books. There were even a few quiet literally sleeping on the engine decks. They were home. I envied them in a way; I hadn't been in the military long enough to really bond within a unit as such. The events of the last few days had really messed things up. I could only hazard a guess of where the other guys from my barrack block were now. If they were not already prisoners, they most certainly would be dead. Such a waste of youth. I now had to deal with my route home. I would have to leave here, and make my way carefully into Kohlstadt. With a bit of luck, the Americans had not moved into there just yet, and if they had, I would have to get past them somehow. It would be a dangerous route home, the Americans could well be in the mood to shoot at anything that moved.

I made my way up to the front of the column; the Commanding Officer was still leaning over the bonnet of his Kubelwagon, studying his map. I just waited for him to finish, whatever he was looking at. My presence caught his eye.

'Young Erik, you still here?' his face was all smiles.

'I wanted to thank you again for letting me go Sir.' I held out my hand. He received it with both hands.

'Erik, go home. You never were under my command in the first place. Besides, these goons are not in a rush to leave, so I will stay to see them off.'

He released his iron grip, and went back to studying his map. My curiosity got the better of me.

'Where is home for you Sir?'

'Seelow.' His head slowly turning to face me. I didn't have a clue where Seelow was. My blank expression must have prompted him to fill me in.

'In the east, in Russian hands.' He peered back down at the map. I felt such a fraud being literally on the door step of my hometown.

'I'm sorry Sir.'

He looked at me with a stern gaze.

' Erik, what have you got to be sorry for? You didn't create this mess. None of us here did. But it's us that must pay for it. History will not be kind to Germany, you do realise that. We will all pay dearly for what has happened in the last six years. So much suffering, and for what? Look where it has got us Erik.'

His eyes were glazed, his lips trembling. I was starting to feel uncomfortable in his company. He stood up straight, reached out and put a gentle hand on my shoulder.

'Erik, you must ensure you get home safely. Promise me, I would like to at least have done some good in this awful war.' He was starting to lose it. I nodded convincingly.

'I promise Sir.' It was me now trying to hold it together.

He broke into a broad tight lipped grin, which cause the dam to break, sending tears rolling down his cheeks.

'Go Erik, be careful how you get past the Americans, like I said, they are unpredictable.'

I shook his hand once more, and turned away. As I stepped away from the column, I was suddenly overwhelmed with loneliness. The boys that remained with the column were with family as such. My guess was they were just waiting for the Americans to take them into custody. I followed the road that would eventually lead me into Kohlstadt. It was early dawn now; it was easier to pick out Kohlstadt as it sat in a deep gorge of sorts. It was cold, but that was the least of my concerns right now. I wanted to get home. Providing I didn't get shot by trigger happy, nervous Americans, I would either get home, or captured. In just shirt, trousers, and boots I had nothing on me to indicate I was SS. That could well go in my favour, if they thought I was just some wandering Werhmacht soldier. I decided to remain on the main road that led me down into the gorge. All was quiet, nothing to be overly concerned about. As I made my way into the outskirts of Kohlstadt, I could see white bed sheets fluttering from almost every window. The residents clearly did not want to resist the invader, and who could blame them.

You could be forgiven if you had the feeling it was all stating to ease off, the war that is. As I passed the first of the houses, they were immaculate, gardens all picture perfect. The war had not ruined this town. Even the bed sheets fluttering above me were brilliant white. Everything was perfect. I just hoped Bad Lipspringge still looked postcard perfect. I was almost halfway through the town when I detected movement up ahead. My stomach turned as I looked desperately for somewhere to hide. I leaped over into the gardens to my left and crawled behind some bushes that marked where the garden ended and the footpath began. I peered through, and to my relief I could see some women pulling an empty cart along. Their children running, jumping and skipping around their feet. I felt it was wise to just stay where I was for the time being and let them pass. I wasn't too confident about the mood they were in. They could be friendly, or they could report me to the nearest American unit, who knew? They went about their business, and I emerged back onto the path, and continued on my way.

I was almost at the southern end of the town when I could make out the rooftops of Schlangen. I knew first hand that the Americans were there. Or at least they were the other day. Fortunately, Bad Lip sat on the far left corner of Schlangen as I was looking at it. What did please me was off to my left was lots of open farmland. I could venture out wide and avoid Schlangen altogether. I moved off the road and made my way through gardens, clucking chickens, and the odd yapping bloody dog, and out into the hedgerows and ditches. As I carefully picked my way through the fields, my mind started to wander. Every time I popped up on a wire strand fence to get my bearings, I would see the girl. We didn't have to kill her. That bastard Dieter enjoyed it no doubt. If there was a Dieter in every village and town filled with the enemy, Germany would be a very dark place for some time to come. It couldn't be long now before it was over. One way or the other, the killing must end soon surely?

The route was painfully slow, but vital. I couldn't afford to drift near Schlangen. What suddenly filled me with dread was the fact that if Schlangen was still occupied by the Americans, then Bad Lip must be. I had not considered it at all on my walk home until now. There wasn't much I could do about it anyhow. Should I wait till dark? Take my chances then? I clambered up onto a fence to get a feel for where abouts I was, Schlangen was as good as off to my right now. I was confident that, if I continued on for a little bit further, I could then strike a straight line into Bad Lip. Not far now Erik, just don't rush it. Getting through the hedges and over the fences was not that easy. The brambles that bordered most of the fields ripped my shirt badly. Every so often I would climb over, and then spend the next two minutes picking myself free from the thorns. The effort of the walk caused me to perspire, which in turn kept the cold at bay. There was a break in the clouds, the sun beamed through and felt fantastic on my face. In the far distance, it glimmered on the little lakes that sat on the outskirts of my neighbourhood. It was like a mirage in the desert. So close, Erik, so close. I took my time to scan the ground ahead of me for anything that could cause me a problem. That main problem would be Americans. Nothing. Had they moved on further into Germany? Or were they hunkered down in the town? I couldn't tell. From what I could make out, there was no evidence of fighting in Bad Lip. No burning houses. They all looked in good shape actually. I could make out the white bed sheets flapping from upstairs windows. No fighting here please. As I scanned further to my left, I could see Paderborn still smouldered. Such a beautiful city, I hoped she could be fixed after all this nonsense was over.

Happy with the fact that I was almost there, I pressed on home. I made sure I didn't rush into anything. Being cautious was good, but it made progress outrageously slow. I fought with all my willpower the urge just to break into a childish sprint and run straight to my front door. The lakes did not seem to be getting any closer. Between them was a narrow strip of land. I used to play around these lakes but a couple of years ago. Willi and Manfred would take me there when they had leave, and we would swim. I missed Willi. Such a waste. I just hoped Manfred had been in touch with mother in my absence. I'm sure there were thousands of families all over Germany fretting over their loved ones. It wasn't just those who went to fight that they worried for, since the war was now in our streets, so to speak, it engulfed everyone. It must surely be over soon.

Before long, I was just short of the lakes. I could almost see the roof of my house in the streets behind. I felt going straight between the lakes was unwise. Should I draw attention to myself, I would be restricted on where I could run. I decide to take a left hook around both of them. This would keep me in the fields, whereas the right side took me next to houses, literally. As I made my way around, I anxiously kept trying to locate my house in the streets beyond. I paused behind some bushes and got a grip of myself. I should be looking out for the enemy, not the fucking chimney stack of my home. I had completed moving around the lakes and carefully made my way in through the first row of houses. Nothing suspicious there. Neat, tidy, white bed sheets out in force. As I picked my way through the gardens, I noticed it was strangely quiet. Nothing out of the ordinary, but I was used to getting the shit scared out of me by clucking chickens or snapping dogs. All I needed to do now was get through the next row of gardens, since the properties backed onto each other, and get through the house. I would then be in my street. Don't rush this Erik. As I moved between the houses, my heart almost failed when a baby suddenly started crying. I felt suddenly sick and had to sit down to compose myself. As I got myself sorted in my neighbours' alleyway, I felt I should at least smarten myself up abit. I tucked my shirt in, made sure my trousers hung properly and my braces were untwisted. I rubbed my boots on the back of my opposite thigh to bring on a shine, why on earth I felt this necessary is anyone's' guess, old habits I suppose. I peered out into my street, confident there wasn't an American armour column having a street party there, I took in the scene. Besides the white bed sheets, all looked as I remembered it as I went off for basic training. Beautiful. I felt a lump rise up in my throat. You are home Erik.

I politely and quietly walked out into my street. My home was in full view. Still nice and tidy, just how mother liked it. I made my way through my garden and stopped just short of the front door. Our front door sat at the side of the house opposite our neighbours' in almost a mirror image of each other. Mine was on the left. I stood before my front door, and I suddenly felt a stranger. Do I ring the bell? Knock on the door? Or just walk straight in? I dismissed bounding straight in, not wanting to give the woman a heart attack. I looked up; she must have used all the bed sheets, since all the upstairs windows had one flapping from it. I closed my eyes, clenched my fist, leaned forward and knocked. Why is it whenever you knock on someone's door, those few seconds before the door open, feel like the longest ever? I was suddenly overwhelmed with worry that she had fled the fighting, and could be anywhere. I knocked again. I could just make out the clatter of shoes on the tiled foyer floor we had. The top bolt crashed across, then the bottom one. The main handle began to turn, the door creaked open. Silver hair, tied up in a bun appeared around the door. Her eyes squinted as she adjusted to the light outside. Her little face came into full view. I had only been here last but a few weeks ago on leave. It felt like a lifetime. She looked at me wearily, her face suddenly changed when she realised this scruffy, half dressed soldier at her door was in fact her youngest son.

'Erik?' her voice quiet and gentle. I nodded, I wanted to speak, but my voice failed me. The door opened wider, her tiny frame was fully clothed, less an overcoat of course. She stepped outside the threshold, holding out her little hands towards mine. I took her hands in mine, so small yet very rough to the touch. Mother was never one for pampering herself at the best of times. Her eyes glazed instantly, the dams on the verge of breaking. I couldn't keep myself together. I welled up; her small hand stroked my cheek.

'My little Erik' she croaked, 'I thought I had lost all my boys.'

I turned my head and kissed her hand. I felt like a little boy in a big, bad mans' world. She stepped forward and embraced me around my midriff. She wasn't very tall, I pushed my tear soaked face into her hair, I could smell soap, fresh and clean. I didn't want to let go of her. Her shoulders bounced as she sobbed into my chest. We remained like this for ages. I was home; home appeared in one piece, I was so grateful to the Americans for not turfing my mother out into the river of refugees also fleeing the fighting. I thanked silently our own masters for not making a stand in these streets. We just remained attached to each other; the only sound in the neighbourhood was the fluttering of bed sheets.

Mother released her tight embrace and looked up at me. 'Is it over Erik?'

'I don't know,' I admitted, 'I really don't know'.

She took a step back, wiping the palms of her hands over her tear streaked face. 'I so want it to be over Erik, this madness has gone on for too long.'

I nodded in agreement. I would like to think the entire country had enough of this madness. I took the risk of upsetting her once more, but I had to ask.

'Anything from Manfred?'

She shook her head, 'nothing, last letter I had, he was in Russia, and that was before you went to basic training'. That country was so vast; you could lose another whole country in there. I had a feeling that he was dead long ago, but I wouldn't dare put my theory to this tiny woman before me. Losing Willi in France shattered my mother, I had to at least let her grip onto the hope that Manfred could still be out there somewhere, trying to get home. She reached forward, taking my hands again, eyeing me up and down.

'You look terrible Erik.' Shaking her head slowly in disapproval.

'Thanks' I chuckled, the mood felt much lighter. She waved me in as she turned to enter the house.

'I will run you a bath, so you can get out of those filthy clothes.' She turned to speak again, her face one of horror.

'ERIK!' she screamed.

I didn't see or hear it coming.

As the world swam back into focus, my head throbbed outrageously. I could hear muffled shouting and screaming, it became more acute, as I gathered myself. I was flat on my back, my right ear cold on the floor tiles of my house. I lifted my heavy head, and what greeted me was one thing I had never imagined. My mother was on her knees, face bleeding and bruised, a soldier stood over her, his hand gripping her hair roughly, as he struck her across the face once more. The soldier went to strike her again, but hesitated, and he dropped her like a sack, spinning around to focus on me. Thomas' eyes were full of hate as he glared at me.

'You thought you could just run away you little fuck!' he roared stampeding towards me. I lifted my knees up to my chest, to aid keeping my distance, as I scrambled backwards. I could only go so far, since the cellar stairs were directly behind me. I grabbed me by my shirt, along with flesh which screamed though my body. Grabbing my hair also, he ripped me from the floor and hauled me back towards mother and the front door. She scrambled to her feet to bar his way, he raised his right boot, ploughing it into her face with all his strength, her face burst in red mist as her tiny inert frame crumpled in the doorway. I roared into his face.

'You fucking bastard, you dare touch my mother!' I was cut short as his forehead smashed into the bridge of my nose. My world faded, sparkles all over the place. He released his grasp, allowing gravity to take care of me.

'Silence, you cowardly turd!' he spat at me,' First I'm going to string up this Jewish whore, then I'm going to have fun with you.' As her went to grab mother, a little hand went up in protest. He flicked her arm away, and dealt her a blow to the head. Her whole body went limp. I clambered to my feet as he turned to confront me. I rhino charged him, full on in the gut. He let out an almighty grunt, as I took the air from his lungs. We both crashed into the door frame, my head once more in the wrong place, taking the majority of the impact. The sparkles returned. I ran out of steam quickly, as Thomas got the better of me. He shoved me back, I went top heavy and staggered back as I tried to stay on my feet, but the opposite doorstep took my feet from me as I crashed against the door. Before I could react, Thomas was on top of me, pinning me down, hands clasped tight around my throat. I grabbed his wrists, and with all what remained of my strength tried to prise them away so I could breathe.

Thomas was not a small man, he was solid and powerful. He was well on his way to squeezing the life out of me. I was losing feeling in my hands, and my whole world was fading once more. The pressure around my neck was overwhelming; I just couldn't summon the strength to release his grip.

The pressure eased off instantly, along with an ear splitting thud. Thomas went limp on me suddenly, making catching my breath very difficult. He coughed and gargled away in my face. I rocked left and right just to get some leverage to get him off me. I managed to roll him off me, his head slamming down on the hard doorstep. Life and air rushed back into my lungs, as I took in great gulps, coughing uncontrollably with each intake of the precious air. Next to me, Thomas was on his back, head propped up by the stone step, mouth full of blood, chin coated in the red liquid that bubbled from every breath he took. His breathing was shallow, his eyes still open and bloodshot. I was overwhelmed by the aroma of human shit, and strong urine. I was confident it wasn't me. I wasn't too sure about Thomas. I rolled away from Thomas onto my side. My head still spun like I had been drunk. I propped myself up on my right elbow, and saw mother, slumped in the doorway, face bloodied and bruised. In her lap, still smoking, a Mauser rifle. Standard military issue. She had taken care of Thomas. Tougher than she looked.

I sat myself upright, head swimming. My legs would just not respond to my wishes. I must have looked pathetic as I crawled over to my bloodied and broken mother. As I scrambled over to her, she tossed the rifle to one side. My head drew level with her thighs; her little rough hand cupped my left ear, and invited me to rest my battered head in her lap. I tried to be polite, but I ended up with the entire weight of my head and shoulders in her lap. Exhaustion was getting the better of me. When I was little, just before bedtime, me and my brothers would sit in front of the fire with mother, all of us a bathed and clean. Me being the youngest, I would have my head in her lap, and she would play with my ear. I found It so relaxing, I would drift off. She would then cart me up to bed without me realising it. With her little hand stroking my ear, I felt so at peace. The spluttering and gargling coming from Thomas distracted me from my slumber. I lifted my head to look at him, but my mother wouldn't allow me too.

'Shush,' she soothed in my ear, 'let him go'

Thomas was in a bad way. The bullet must have smashed his spine, since only his upper torso was able to move. The blood around his lower back and buttocks was dark, and starting to congeal and dry. He was trying to reach around behind him, but now paralysed from the waist down, he couldn't achieve it. All he could do was lay in his own shit and piss, and allow life to drain out of him. With a splutter and a gargle, he drew his elbows up tight alongside his chest and clumsily propped himself up. Fixing mother and I a hateful stare.

'It's because of weak people like you, Germany is in this position.' He managed to gasp amongst the blood bubbles. I went to bark back at him, but mother placed a small gentle hand over my mouth.

'You are right my dear,' she whispered gently back at him.' For allowing men like you to lead Germany into this position.'

His glare suddenly dropped, he hadn't banked on such a quick answer from the battered little woman. In sheer contempt, he spat his blood at us, and slumped back on the step. The gargling and groaning continued. Thomas refused to die. I felt mothers little fingers run through my filthy, matted hair.

'Let's get you inside and cleaned up.' She whispered. Remarkable, this little woman had almost been killed, and her only concern was sorting me out. I lifted my delicate head from her lap. She managed to get herself to her feet, and then help me up. Still abit unsteady on my feet, we began to make our way inside.

'Woman!' barked a blood gargling Thomas.' Since I doubt your boy is up to it, feel free to end my war for me.'

I just wanted to storm outside and finish him off, but mother grasped my arm and told me to stay where I was. She stepped back outside and made her way over to Thomas' foul inert frame slumped against the neighbours step. Ensuring she was out of his reach, she knelt down next to him.

'What is your name young man?' She was gentle in her manner.

Thomas merely glared back at her, 'what the fuck has that got to do anything?'

Mother remained passive,' what harm could it do to be properly introduced?'

Thomas' glare relaxed slightly, 'Thomas, my name is Thomas.'

Mother stood back up, still smiling and courteous, 'well let me tell you what we are all going to do now Thomas', she paused ' we are all going to sit tight, and wait for this horrible war to be over, including you.'

With that, she made her way back into the house, as she slowly closed the door; we were subject to Thomas' last defiant gesture.

'You fucking Jewish whore!'

With the door shut, the foyer was dark. Mother shuffled over to one of the lamps. The soft glow emitted from it as she lit it gave off an amazing feeling of homeliness and warmth.

'What do we do now?' I asked. She smiled at me.

'We wait for the Americans; there is nothing else we can do'.

# EPILOGUE

The Americans did come, but not for me. I remained upstairs when then knock at the door came. I peered through the nets that covered the window. There was an American patrol in the street. I looked down over our courtyard. Thomas had been there about two days now. I don't think he made it through the first night. The American in charge was talking through an interpreter, who happened to be another German soldier. Mother explained that she thought it was an American patrol that shot him, and was therefore too scared to go out and investigate. Mother had placed the Mauser rifle just out of Thomas' grasp not too long after we had closed the door on him. She was asked about how she obtained her facial injuries. She told them she had to fight off some looters the other night. The Americans appeared satisfied with my mothers' explanation, and called up one of their big trucks to take the body away.

Whilst I enjoyed my first bath at home in front of the fire, mother took what was left of my uniform and put it in the fire. The only things that refused to burn were the hobnails on the soles of my boots. I had to have a few baths that evening, since the grime I was coated in was unrelenting. Once cleaned and dressed in a lose shirt and trousers, mother and I tended to each other's wounds. We would both recover, my mother's broken nose was the only real injury sustained. Being at home was a great feeling, but also one of nervousness. I kind of expected at any moment for the Americans to do house searches for hiding soldiers. Or for the SS or our own Military police to come back into town and enforce their policies back upon us.

Mother insisted that I stay indoors for the foreseeable future since no one actually knew if the war was over, and me being of fighting age, I could well be interned. Fighting age, that was a joke in itself. In those last weeks of the war, if you could fire a weapon you were of fighting age.

Germanys' source of fighting men was hardly vast in 1945, let it be said. Food was a problem for a while, since the Americans had to not only feed their armies, and their prisoners, they were tasked with helping get the civilian population away from the brink of starvation. Potatoes and vegetables were the stable diet for some time. Bread wasn't too hard to come by; I think many people made their own. Mother's bread was satisfactory, but it did the job. I can't exactly remember when meat was back on the menu. The Americans didn't stay around too long, they moved further into Germany, a clear indicator that it was not all over just yet. I remember one afternoon; mother came back from wherever she would go, and called me downstairs. She was full of smiles.

The German Army had formerly surrendered.

A huge wave of relief washed over me. Yes, it was clear we had been defeated, but it meant as far as we were concerned, there would be no more fighting. I went out into the street. The white sheets still fluttered like flags, but to be outside in the world again was an awesome feeling. The street was very quiet, losing the war was not a cause for celebration, but I defy anyone on that day, German or otherwise who wasn't happy that the fighting had ended.

Over the next few months or so. Mother was happy and sad in equal measure. The former fighting men of Germany were being released and coming home. Slowly, those men from Bad Lip, and Paderborn in general were present on the streets once more. These were the guys that had been taken prisoner by the British, Americans, French and Canadians. The boys from Russia had not yet returned. I heard of some men talking about their time in America, working as farm labourers. No fences, no watchtowers, just in the middle of America. My thoughts drifted to those still in the middle of Russia. Was Manfred amongst them? I would have given anything for my mother to receive a letter confirming Manfred was alive. The not knowing was the worst part of it all.

Paderborn was in a real bad way. Her rail yard and roads were shattered beyond recognition. Unless you were skilled in building or engineering, you didn't have a job as such. Unemployment was a big problem for some time after the war. We had food, that wasn't the problem, but money was very rare in these parts. Just to get me out of the house, I would volunteer to work in Paderborn clearing out the wrecked areas. My job, as trite as it may seem, was to collect what bricks were intact and stack them on the back of a horse drawn cart. For use in the rebuild, whenever that happened. Unexploded bombs were a problem, and there were some tragedies to go with the risky nature of our work. I only did the clear up work for a short while, when I was offered a job as a farm labourer just outside Schlangen. The money wasn't movie star wages, but mother and I were grateful for it all the same.

Years had passed when the first boys from Russia were finally released. They were empty shells of men. Old before their time. Hard labour in Siberia had made them that way. I'm not asking for sympathy with regards to how our guys were treated, since we had much to be ashamed of during those dark years, but these guys looked terrible. Mother would approach these men as they waited for buses or drank coffee in cafes by the roadside. Thousands of men fought in Russia, I felt her efforts were all in vain, but I couldn't bring myself to tell her. If he wasn't dead, there was still a chance.

Over the years, we began to see an improvement in how Paderborn was shaping up. I was so grateful that my hometown had not been mauled by the fighting. I was still working on the farm, wages had got a little better, and Mother was not quite so active those days. I returned home from work one evening, mother was at the large table in the kitchen, tears streaming down her face, gripping a letter. She kept kissing the letter, and rubbing her cheek with it. She looked up at me, face full of smiles, cheeks smeared in ink, but unable to speak. All she did was wave the letter at me, imploring me to read. It was letter headed from the Red Cross. As I tried my best to read around the smears, it became apparent that my mother's prayers had been answered. Manfred was alive. He was currently in Berlin, under medical and nutritional supervision, and would be arriving in Paderborn Bahnhof in the next few days. I burst into tears, as my not so frail mother sprung to her feet and embraced me. Thank you, thank you, thank you.

It was great to have Manfred home. He looked a little rough around the edges, and certainly underweight, but apart from that, it was fantastic to have him back. My boss on the farm gave me the next day off to spend time with him, and even handed me a few small bottles of beer, what a nice guy. Once we had eaten, and mother had kissed us both goodnight, we settled down with the beers and told each other our adventures. I went first; they were rather tame in comparison to his. I didn't tell him about the girl, or the American at the roadblock. As far as he was concerned, I escaped from the American artillery and joined another unit in Horn. His stories were far more chilling. What he told me about Russia also confirmed what Bobby had told me that night we were on watch together in Borchen. What did make me uncomfortable were his stories of being a prisoner in Siberia. The Russians didn't waste trucks and fuel on their prisoners, they walked. Anyone that couldn't keep up was shot on the spot. He went on to say that once they got to wherever 'there' was, they had to then build the camp themselves. Frozen and starving, their captors threw some axes and saws' in the snow and told them to find the materials to build their camp. There was a forest about a kilometre away, and would have to drag the fallen trees back to the spot where it was to be built. It took weeks he said. Hundreds perished in the snow. Once done, the Russians didn't feel the need to build a wire fence, since there was nothing in either direction. My war lasted merely days; I felt abit of a fraud.

We talked about Willi. Willi was killed at a place called Falaise, that's all I knew. Over the years, I have read many history books about the Battle of Normandy. Falaise was the epicentre of destruction of the German Army in France. The only units to make it out of France were badly mauled. By the time it came to fight in Paderborn, our army was nothing more than old men, young boys, and some experienced Officers and NCOs' expected to win the war. Old men and children, fighting on all sides of Germany, expected to defeat all we encountered. Total madness. If anything has been learnt from the war, it must be warnings to those who in future want follow the beliefs of one bitter and twisted man into a world of chaos.

Time marches on. Mother is no longer with us. Manfred passed away not too long ago. My children now have their own children. How Germany has changed. Full of promise again, not in a menacing way, but as a nation, we are an economical force. We have our issues, the EU, immigration, same as most other countries. My sons served their National Service in the Bundeswehr, they hated it. They did their basic training, then one of them when to Somalia peacekeeping, the other went to Kosovo to do pretty much the same. My grandchildren are taught about 'The Holocaust' in school. It is something we must not be allowed to forget, but I do feel sorry for our teenagers these days. People like to ram it down their throats when it suits them. Don't blame our children, blame their grandparents, we are the ones to blame. On the news now and then we hear of some war criminal being arrested in South America or somewhere exotic like that. If I may be so bold as to make an observation. The main ring leaders of all that was terrible all that time ago are now long dead. It appears to me that those groups who dedicate their lives to tracking people down are now clutching at straws. Just because that old man manned that watchtower when he was a boy does not make him the murderer of innocents.

Every night I go to bed, I think of the girl.

Every night, I fear the Nazi hunters.

Printed in Great Britain
by Amazon